John Thelwall

Sober reflections on the seditious and inflamatory Letter of
the Right Hon

John Thelwall

Sober reflections on the seditious and inflamatory Letter of the Right Hon

ISBN/EAN: 9783337103361

Printed in Europe, USA, Canada, Australia, Japan

Cover: Foto ©Andreas Hilbeck / pixelio.de

More available books at **www.hansebooks.com**

SOBER REFLECTIONS

ON THE

SEDITIOUS AND INFLAMMATORY

LETTER

OF

THE RIGHT HON. EDMUND BURKE,

TO

A NOBLE LORD.

ADDRESSED TO THE SERIOUS CONSIDERATION OF HIS

FELLOW CITIZENS,

BY JOHN THELWALL.

" Next Anger rush'd—his eyes on fire,
" In lightnings own his secret stings."

LONDON:

PRINTED FOR H. D. SYMONDS, NO. 20, PATERNOSTER-ROW.

1796.

AS the following pages are intended, in some
fort, as a reply to the inflammatory mifreprefentations and incongruous principles of a
recent pamphlet, from the elegant and abufive
pen of Mr. BURKE, it might have been expected,
perhaps, that I fhould have followed the example
of my antagonift, by throwing my obfervations
into the form of a letter, and addreffing it either
to fome great perfonage, or to that antagonift
himfelf. But it has long been a principle with
me, that, as far as it is practicable, at leaft, in
the ftate of fociety in which we live, our open
profeffion and our real object fhould always be
the fame; and I have been frequently difpofed
to fufpect that all colourable pretences, all habits
of fubterfuge, even in circumftances of the moft
apparent indifference, have a tendency to weaken
the moral feelings, and produce a bias of mind
eminently unfavourable to rectitude of judgment,
and that enthufiaftic attachment to the caufe of
truth, which is, in reality, the nobleft attribute
of a cultivated underftanding. There is a manly

B   and

and independent energy of mind, encouraged by a fcrupulous adherence, not only to the *effence*, but even to the *fhews* and *forms* of fincerity, which a friend of liberty ought to be particularly zealous to preferve. I therefore addrefs thefe animadverfions on one of the moft extraordinary pamphlets that ever were publifhed, openly and avowedly to my fellow citizens, for whofe advantage they are principally intended ; and from whom, alone, I have the vanity to expect any confiderable portion of attention: for I have not the fortune (good or bad—as " the zealots of the *old* fect in philo- " fophy and politics *," may choofe to confider it) to be either the penfioned *dependant*, friend, or correfpondant of any noble lord, with whofe honours I might emblazon my title-page ; and, as for Mr. *Burke* himfelf, the diftemper of his mind is fo evident in every thing which of late years he has either faid or written, that it is impoffible to expect from him the fmalleft degree of candid attention to the arguments of one whom, upon no better evidence than the fuggeftions of his own furious prejudices, he ftigmatifes as " a " wicked pander to avarice and ambition†." The hydrophobia of alarm rages too fiercely in his mind, to fuffer him to wet his lips with the fober ftream of reafon, or turn to the falutary

* Letter, &c. p. 1.   Ibid, p. 47.

food

food of impartial inveftigation. All is rage, and foam, and headlong precipitancy; and the individual muft be as mad as himfelf who expects any thing but to be torn by his invenomed tooth, from an attempt to ftop him in his career, or turn him to the right, or to the left, to examine the grounds over which he is fo furioufly running.

Let me, however, be underftood: I apply this metaphor not in the bitternefs of malevolence, but in the kindnefs of pity. I would not willingly—even if my feeble lance were capable of piercing the feven-fold fhield of literary and ariftocratic pride by which my oponent is defended,— I would not wantonly tear with frefh wounds, a breaft already bleeding with the keeneft anguifh of paternal affliction.

Mr. *Burke* does not, perhaps, expect fo much candour and moderation from one whofe principles are diametrically oppofite to his own; and who does not even fhrink from the imputation of being a *Democrat*, a *Jacobin*, or a *Sans Culotte:* [for it is too much the habit with the violent of all parties, to fuppofe that there can be nothing virtuous or liberal in the character of any man who is of an oppofite principle to themfelves:] yet when I perufe the pathetic paffage in this beautiful, but mifchievous letter, *I feel*, though prejudice may not *believe*, that I can fympathife

B 2   with

with the afflictions of an enemy; even when, from that perverfion, from which the fineft under-ftandings are not exempt, he happens, according to my judgement, to be the enemy, alfo, of the human race. In one refpect, alfo, I have ever been ambitious of emulating the *chivalrous fpirit* of our ancient heroes. I can venerate the talents and enthufiafm employed againft my own caufe; and (in the more liberal acceptation of the phrafe) as *Shakefpere* expreffes it—

" *Envy* their great defervings and high merits,
" Becaufe they are not of our determination,
" But ftand againft us as an enemy."

I fhould not, therefore, exult if Mr. *Burke's* "*feelings*" were, in reality, what he calls them, " nearly extinguifhed*;" I do not exult to find them, on the contrary, the moft irritable that ever burned (like a hot-ach) under the froft of age: far lefs do I exult in thofe incongruities of mind, which exhibit reafon in its dotage, while the imagination is ftill rioting in all the vigour and luxuriancy of youth. I bow with veneration to the gigantic powers of his unwearied intellect; I gaze with rapture upon the fplendid effufions of his inexhauftible fancy; and I have not the favage ignorance to fuppofe that if I had the will,

* Letter, &c. p. 2.

or

or the power, to deftroy his reputation, I could transfer his genius to myfelf, or plant his honours upon my own brow. Nor, indeed, when the fubjeét is weighed in the important fcale of effeéts and confequences, have the friends of liberty any ferious caufe to lament his exertions. The provocation of political difcuffion is the grand defideratum for political improvement: and, fo far is the gall of perfonal animofity from my pen, that, in the fervent fincerity of foul, I can exclaim—" Far, far may that period be removed, when fate or caprice fhall inflịét upon him either the filence of death, or the death of filence!"

I could wifh, indeed, that a mind fo rich, fo cultivated, fo powerful, were upon the fide of truth: but if he will but write, take whatever fide he will, I am fure that truth will be derived from his labours: for I defy Mr. *Burke*, or any other individual of penetrating and energetic mind, under what unfortunate delufion foever he may labour, to publifh a pamphlet of eighty pages, without bringing forward fome important obfervations, which, on account of their firm foundation in juftice, will remain, while thofe which are falfe will be expofed and rejeéted by the difcuffion which fuch publications cannot fail of producing. Nay, the very abfurdities and fophifms of a vigorous mind are fubfervient to juft conclufion: for, from the energy with which

they

they are expreffed, they take faft hold upon
the imagination, and compell the reflecting reader
to give them that repeated revifion which,
unlefs the mind is very confiderably warped by
the ftrong bias of interefted prejudice, cannot fail
of conducting the enquirer to principles of liberty
and juftice.

In this point of view, the caufe of liberty has
effential obligations to the pen of Mr. *Burke*. He
has written books which have converted fuch of
his *difintere/ted* readers, as were in the habit of
thinking for themfelves, *from* the caufe he endeavoured to uphold, *to* that which it was his object
to overthrow; he has provoked anfwers, which,
extending the boundaries of fcience beyond the
narrow pale of opulence, have carried the invaluable difcuffion of political principles and civil
rights to the fhopboard of the artificer, and the
cottage of the laborious hufbandman; and his
ungovernable phrenzy has hurried him into *expreffions* and *epithets* fo repugnant to every principle of juftice and humanity*, and fo revoltingly
difgufting to the common fympathies of nature,
as could not fail of producing a very general con-
viction, I will not fay, as fome have faid, of the
rottennefs of his heart (for who fhall judge of the
motives of man, or fet bounds to the omnipotency

* Reflections, &c.

of

of felf-delufion!) but of the weaknefs and injuftice of that caufe which could reduce fuch talents to the neceffity of appealing to weapons fo grofs and fo unmanly.

In this laft fpecies of warfare the fury of my prefent antagonift has been at leaft fufficiently feconded by the *metaphyfical* phrenzy of his friend Mr. *Windham.* Indeed, if this *gentleman* had been *hired by the Jacobins of France to difguft all ranks of people* (placemen, penfioners, and dependants alone excepted) *with the laws, government, and conftitution of this country*, he could not have proceeded to more wanton infults upon their feelings. To fay nothing of his quotation, and direct application of that line from *Shakefpere,*

" If *Richard's* fit to live, let *Richmond* fall:

Which, if it meant any thing, was referring the queftion to this bloody arbitrement—*either thefe reformers ought to die by the hands of government, or the governing party by the hands of the reformers;*—what fhall we fay to " acquitted felons," " killed off," and a variety of other fentences, of whofe " *vitality*" this fubtile, Machievelian fecretary (terrified by the lingering echo of his own frenzy) has fo pathetically complained? It is difficult to conceive how human nature could become callous enough to give utterance to thefe, and other expreffions, ftill more inhuman, of which I fhall have occafion to take notice:

But

but Mr. *Burke*, in the very pamphlet I am anfwering, furnifhes us, according to his conception, at leaft, with a fufficient explanation. " Nothing can be conceived," fays he, " more " hard than the heart of a thorough-bred meta- " phyfician. It comes nearer to the cold malig- " nity of a wicked fpirit, than to the frailty and " paffion of a man. It is like that of the prin- " ciple of evil himfelf, incorporeal, pure, un- " mixed, dephlegmated, defecated evil*."

In what particular country Mr. *Burke* has met with thofe philofophers and metaphyficians, from whofe example he has drawn this definition, I fhall enquire more particularly hereafter; and on the validity of his arguments, in this refpect, I may perhaps be admitted to decide with the greater impartiality, from having the misfortune (for fuch I believe it is, to be deficient in any branch of knowledge) of being liable to no part of that rancorous animofity, with which he is *fometimes* difpofed to regard both the fcience and the profeffors of metaphyfics. In the mean time, that I may not appear to prejudge the queftion, permit me to declare, that, if it can be fhewn that thefe fubtile difquifitions and abftract enquiries are neceffarily hoftile to the principles and practice of humanity, I fhall hold myfelf in readi-

* Letter, &c. p. 61.

nefs

nefs to reject with equal abhorrence " the philo-
" fophy that would eradicate the beft feelings of
" the heart," and that fyftem of private attachment and obligation, which, preferring a part to
the whole, would facrifice to *individual gratitude*
the interefts and happinefs of mankind!

But the moft powerful of thofe champions, for
whofe efforts in behalf of liberty we are indebted
to the ungovernable fury of Mr. *Burke*'s attacks,
have not been found either among the metaphyficians, or the ferocious violators of the principles
of humanity. The ftrong, rude, fometimes incoherent, but always gigantic mind of *Thomas
Paine*, had been neither fafhioned nor debauched
by the fubtilties nor the fophiftries of metaphyfics; and he has approved, at the peril of his
life, the fettled averfion of his foul, not only to
the maffacres, tumultuary or legal, which have
difgraced the *French Revolution*, but even to that
" penal retrofpect" which rendered the faith-
lefs and perjured Louis a victim to the trea-
cherous duplicity with which he confpired for
the deftruction of his people. And as for
thofe other diftinguifhed antagonifts of Mr.
Burke, whom this country may more exclufively
challenge as her own; they are men whofe focial
virtues have either never yet been queftioned,
or being queftioned, have been put to the-ordeal,

C   and

and paſſed, like pure gold, through the fire, undiminiſhed either in weight or luſtre.

The energy of ſome of the moſt celebrated of theſe has, it is true, been relaxed awhile, by the enervating influence of party attachment; while others, infected by the temporary mania of alarm, have *appeared*, at leaſt, to deſert the ſacred cauſe: but let the tools and advocates of corruption beware; for if tyranny ſhould advance with too audacious a ſtride—if thoſe who have already provoked ſo much difcuſſion, encouraged by a temporary ſupineneſs, ſhould inſult too outrageouſly the feelings and underſtandings of the nation, theſe champions may be provoked to reſume their neglected arms, or others, ſtill more irreſiſtible, may ſtep forward to ſupply their place. The manly ſpirit of Britain is not dead but ſleepeth. Sampſon in the lap of Dalila *(the Dalila of dependance and corruption!)* ſlumbers it is true, amidſt his bonds: but he is not yet ſhorn of his ſtrength; nor is the myſtic ſecret yet diſcovered: and ſhould he chance but to awaken from his lethargy, the *new cords* may be burſt aſunder, and the *Philiſtines* be compelled to fly!

Behold then the unwearied ſervices of *Edmund Burke*, whom corruption has penſioned for its own deſtruction! who defends the privileged orders

orders by overwhelming their privileges with contemptuous ridicule! and protects the inviolability of places and penfions, by tearing afunder the venerable veil of prefcription, and undermining the foundations of hereditary property!

But what reafon foever the noble perfonages attacked in this letter may have to hurl back the charge upon their affailant, and accufe the *miniflerial faction* of being " executors in their " own wrong*," the friends of popular enquiry " have nothing to complain of."—" It is well! " it is perfectly well! *We* have to do homage† " to" his zeal in the caufe of political invefti-gation.

The difcuffion provoked by his inconfiderate " Reflections" was nearly exhaufted; the *nine days wonder* of the State Trials had fubfided; political perfecution had become familiar, and, like the daily bread of a land in plenty, was taken as matter of courfe, and digefted without comment or obfervation; and whatever fpirit or energy had hitherto remained among the people, feemed to have evaporated in the ftruggle provoked by Mr. *Pitt*'s and Lord *Grenville*'s bills, and to have left them, in this refpect, like the fallen angels, after the toils of unfuccefsful fight, repofing in the oblivious pool, equally forgetful

---

of the difgrace they had experienced, and of the energies by which it might be retrieved. Mr. *Burke*, however, knew that this was not the ftate in which it was their duty, or their intereft to re-main; and he determined, accordingly, to awaken them from their lethargy. He feized, therefore, again the trump of political controverfy—

> ——————" With a withering look,
> " The war-denouncing trumpet took,
> " And blew a blaft fo loud and dread,
> " *Were ne'er prophetic founds fo full of woe!*
> " And ever and anon he beat
> " *The doubling drum* with furious heat *."

Such a peal, at fuch a time was certainly of all things moft defirable. No other circum-ftance could, perhaps, fo foon, and fo effectually, have revived the energies of popular exertion, or have diffipated fo effectually the lazy mifts of torpor and defpondency which hung on the fickening ear of Britifh virtue, and threatened it with eternal blight: fo true is it that thofe advan-tages which the ardour of friendfhip labours to produce in vain, are frequently conferred by the over-active zeal of our bittereft enemies.

But it will be faid, if fuch is my exultation at the appearance of this letter, why have I called it a " mifchievous pamphlet?" To this I anfwer, that the advantages to be expected from this letter

* Collins.

are

are confequential—certainly not intended; but that the mifchief is in the thing itfelf. Mifchief and good are merely relative terms; for nothing is exclufively productive either of the one or the other: and with refpect to intellectual, or literary exertions, the balance is always eventually, I believe, favourable to the happinefs of mankind. . In fhort, it feems to be paft the time, in this part of Europe at leaft, when it is in the power of any book to be productive of ultimate mifchief. Mankind now read too many books to be permanently injured by any. Whatever mifchief is to be apprehended, muft be rather from the *ftagnation* than the *nature* of their enquiries: and, perhaps, the beft advice that can be given them, is to read every thing that comes in their way, from a Grub-ftreet ballad to a Royal proclamation. There are, however, fome publications which, abftractedly confidered, and independant of thofe anfwers likely to be produced in a bufy, literary, difputatious age, like the prefent, muft be confidered as moft pernicious in their tendency: and fuch, above all that ever fell under my cognizance, is " *A Letter from the Right Honourable Edmund* " *Burke to a Noble Lord.*"

So rafh—fo intemperate—fo imprudent—I cannot help adding, fo *unprincipled* an attack upon the peaceful fecurity of all property, never has been made, I believe, before, fince England had

a language

a language in which that attack could be con-
veyed. Sir *Thomas Moore*, it is true, has vifited
the clofets of fpeculative men with the fafcinat-
ing picture of a fociety in which inceffant toil
is not the portion of any man, and every thing is
enjoyed in common : But there is nothing in the
" *Eutopia*" that is irritating or inflammatory ; nothing that is calculated to hurry the uncultivated
mind into rafh conclufions, or fhake the foundations of fociety with fudden convulfion. *Thomas
Paine*, alfo, in the fecond part of his " Rights of
Man," projected, what *Servius Tullius* partly exe-
cuted in ancient Rome, a fcheme of progreffive
taxation, by which the towering pride of wealth
might be humbled and reftrained, and the burthens of government be fhifted from the poor
man's fhoulders : And *Licinius*, and the much celebrated, and much flandered, *Gracchi* laboured hard
for the eftablifhment of thofe *Agrarian* laws which
conftituted an important article in the original
compact of the Roman government, and muft be
regarded as among the *conftitutional rights* of that
nation. But for Mr. *Burke*, alone, of all the de-
mogogues I ever read or heard of, was referved
the *honourable* diftinction of affailing, with *popular
fury*, the very exiftence of all property ; ftirring
up the paffions of a diftreffed and irritated people, by reprefenting the " overgrown" fortunes
of the nobility as " oppreffing the induftry of
" humble

" humble men *," " trampling on the mediocri-
" ty of humble and laborious individuals †," and
the like.

In fhort, Mr. *Burke* is the firft complete *leveller*
I have met with: the only man who has had the
audacity, in direct and popular language, addreff-
ed at once to the perceptions and paffions of
mankind at large, to reprefent all wealth—all
territorial poffeffion, as plunder and ufurpation
—as the fruit of blood, of treachery, of profcription!—as being obtained by " the murder of
" innocent perfons ‡,"—" from the aggregate
" and confolidated funds of judgments *iniquitoufly*
" *legal!* and from "poffeffions *voluntarily furrendered*
" by the lawful proprietors *with the gibbet at their*
" *door* ‡ ;" nay, to complete the climax, as having been augmented *(as fome fortunes are at this
very day augmenting!)* by " bringing poverty,
" wretchednefs, and depopulation on the coun-
" try §," and fwelled by confifcations produced
" by inftigating a tyrant to injuftice, to provoke
" a people to rebellion §."

I do not ftand forward as the champion of pre-
fcriptive rights, nor wield the fword of reafon
for the perpetuity of ancient prejudices, or the
vindication of hereditary honours. I am more

---

* Letter p. 33.   † Ibid. 39.   ‡ Ibid. p. 42.   § Ibid. p. 44.
and p. 48.

folicitous

folicitous about the living than the dead: more anxious for the happinefs of pofterity than the reputation of long buried anceftors. I leave there-fore to the avowed advocates of the illuftrious and the great, the eafy tafk of repelling a confiderable part, at leaft, of that outrageous obloquy which, though directed againft a particular family, does in reality, more or lefs, befpatter the whole body of the nobility and great proprietors of the land. But, if fuch *were* the real foundations of property—if fuch were indeed the ftuff of which all eftate, and wealth, and grandeur were compofed, what good and confiderate man—what friend to the peace and order of fociety—to the fweet fleep of fecurity, and the humane emotions of the heart, would have laid bare thofe foundations with *fo rude* a ftroke?

There are even fome truths of the utmoft importance to the improvement and happinefs of fociety, which the true philofopher, though he will not fupprefs, will unfold with a tender and a trembling hand. He will proceed with a caution almoft bordering on referve; and will accompany every advance towards the requifite developement with the moft folicitous expofition of every appendage and confequence of the refpective parts of his doctrine; left by pouring acceptable truths too fuddenly on the popular eye, inftead of falutary light he fhould produce
blindnefs

blindnefs and frenzy! and from premifes the moft juft, plunge into conclufions of the moft deftructive nature. Such in particular are many of the fpeculations which relate to the fubject of property. Thefe are indeed of fo delicate a nature—the abufes relating to them are fo clofely interwoven with the very texture of fociety—and the principles upon which they ftand are fo liable to mifapprehenfion and abufe, that it is almoft doubtful whether mankind is yet fufficiently enlightened and humanized for the inveftigation, and whether the fubject had not been as well omitted even in the *abstract and speculative quartos of William Godwin.* For my own part, at leaft, confcious of the difficulty of keeping clear from all dangerous mifapprehenfions, I have never ventured to enter much into the fubject: not but that I can fee with as much clearnefs, and feel with as keen a fympathy, as Mr. *Burke* (when it fuits the purpofes of his political frenzy and perfonal refentments) can himfelf pretend, the vices, the miferies, the unfocial pride and abject wretchednefs too frequently produced in fociety by thofe huge maffes and immeafurable difproportions of property, which unjuft laws and impolitic inftitutions, more than the rapacity of individuals, have tended to accumulate.

Perhaps there is no humane and reflecting man who does not, occafionally at leaft, wifh

D   that

that refpeĉtability were more attached to other things, and lefs to wealth; that the great body of the people were redeemed from that neceffity of unremitting drudgery, penurious food, and confequent ignorance and depreffion of intelleĉt, to which they are fo invariably doomed; and that the huge and unwieldy maffes of wealth and territory (too vaft for enjoyment—too dazzling for juft and prudent diftribution) were in the way of being gradually and peacefully melted down, by the falutary operation of wife and equitable laws. There is perhaps, for example, no one who does not occafionally queftion the juftice of the law of primogeniture—the great root of all the evil; and the propriety of marrying together contiguous and overgrown eftates, without regard to the inclinations, difpofitions, taftes, averfions, and confequent morals of the parties, who are to be the inftruments, or perhaps the viĉtims, of thefe fchemes of family aggrandizement. In fhort, there are undoubtedly a thoufand evils refulting from the prefent ftate of things, in this refpeĉt; and there are perhaps a thoufand palliative remedies that might be applied without lacerating the focial frame, or diffolving the facred ties of reciprocal fecurity and protection. Whatever can be done, in this or any other refpeĉt, for the emancipation of mankind, and the advancement of general happinefs, it is right that we fhould enquire into the means of

doing;

doing ; and the wider the real knowledge of thofe means can be diffeminated, the better for the peace and happinefs of the world. Every thing that relates to this fubject ought, however, I repeat it, to be treated with extreme delicacy and caution ; for there are conclufions fo falfe, and confequences fo terrible, laying within a hair's breadth, as it were, of the truths we aim at, that he who rufhes forward with too boifterous a precipitancy, is in danger of provoking all the horrors of tumult and affaffination ; inftead of ameliorating the condition of the human race. No tricks and arts of eloquence, no gufts of paffion, no inflammatory declamation, nor the leaft incitement to perfonal animofity or refentment, ought to be admitted in the examination of fuch a queftion. It is a new and untried navigation. Almoft all that we know about it is, that the fhoals are dangerous, and the quickfands innumerable. And under fuch circumftances, above all, it muft certainly be the duty of a cautious mariner to " heave the lead every inch of the " way he makes*." But Mr. *Burke*, who, when a few places and penfions were all the freight he had on board, thought thefe precautions neceffary, tears from its moorings the veffel of hereditary property, and, notwithftanding " the aweful ftate

---

* Letter, p. 23.

of

" of the time*," giving the rudder to his refentment, expofes it, at random, to all the fury of the
tempeft which himfelf has raifed.

Is it poffible that Mr. *Burke*'s new patrons
can countenance all this? Has the zeal of his
penfioned gratitude tranfported him too far? Or
is it a part of the long-digefted confpiracy of political panders and rotten borough-mongers? Is
no property to be facred, but the *property of feats
and votes* in the Houfe of Commons? And are
the foundations of all other inheritance to be
fhaken, that thefe ufurpations may be rendered the more fecure, and the authority of the
Steeles and the *Rofes*, who meafure their eftates by
the fquare inch on the planks of St. Stephen's
chapel, be relieved from the checks and counter-
poifes that may hitherto have controuled the
exercife of their fpurious fovereignty?

Let us hope, at leaft, that we are not to look
for the folution of this myftery to fome blacker
caufe. Let us hope, at leaft, that this infidious
new-created *oligarchy* have not, on the profpect
of failure in their ordinary refources, turned to
the *bird's-eye profpect* of new " confifcations of the
" ancient nobility of the land†," to fupport their
all-devouring fyftem of corruption. Let us hope,
at leaft, that this inflammatory farago of denun-

---

* Letter, p. 36.   † Ibid. p. 41.

ciation

ciation and profcription—this portentous retro-
fpeƈt of two hundred and fifty years is not fent
out, as the *avant courier* of a fanguinary faƈion,
to prepare the way for the meditated cataftrophe
of other " innocent perfons of illuftrious rank *,"
whofe fate, according to Mr. *Burke*'s fuperftitious
mode of calculation, might atone for " the but-
" chery of the Duke of *Buckingham* †," and the
" pillage" committed upon that " body of unof-
" fending men *," the *monks* of *Taviftock* and
Wooburn Abbey ‡.

Inflammatory pamphlets, and ferocious fcurri-
lities in the daily prints, have however paved the
way, of late, for attempts equally daring and un-
expeƈed : and the axe, which has paffed over
the humble weeds without inflicting a wound,
may be deftined to try its edge upon the ftatelieft
oaks of the foreft.

Some, perhaps, may put together the circumftances of Mr. *Burke*'s *education*, the pathetic
lamentations which he has poured forth in a former publication§, upon the impious invafion of
the facred flumbers of the cloifter, and the fre-
quent allufions in this pamphlet to the wrongs
of monks and abbots, priefts and Cordeliers, Ca-
puchins, Carmelites, Francifcans, and Domini-
cans‖ ; and hence they may fuppofe, at leaft, that

* Letter, p. 42.   † Ibid. p. 48.   ‡ Ibid p. 68.
§ Refleƈions, &c.   ‖ Letter, p. 41, 42, 43, 67, 68.

they

they have difcovered another reafon for the intemperate zeal of *the pupil of St. Omers*. They
may trace, perhaps, in this bitter and inflexible
malevolence, againft *the inheritor of the crimes of
former centuries*, the feeds of that *metaphyfical piety*,
fo confiftent with the myftical refinements of a
Jefuit's college, which afcribes all the fublime
attributes of the Deity to whatever is connected
with the priefthood, and, of courfe, confiders
the wrongs of that facred order, according to
their own language, as neither paft nor future—
as exifting always in the prefent tenfe—accumu-
lated and concentrated in the ONE ETERNAL
NOW!!!

If, however, we appeal to internal evidence,
we fhall find that motives of a more perfonal nature have not been entirely without influence in
the production of this pamphlet. That unfocial
vanity—that irritable felf-love—that proud im-
patience of queftion or controul, which regards
all oppofition as infult, and " all infult as a
" wound *;"—in fhort, that proud and revengeful
egotifm, which has formed fo diftinguifhing a
trait in the character of all inveterate ariftocrats,
from *Appius Claudius* to *Edmund Burke*, muft be
admitted to have had fomething to do, at leaft,
with the colouring of the piece, to whatever in-

---

* Reflections, &c.

ftigation we may attribute the fketch, or the original defign. What but this could have hurried fuch a man into fuch extravagant inconfiftencies? What but this, even penfioned as he is, could have rendered him fo blind an inftrument to the ufurpations of a faction which he cannot but defpife, and have driven him with fuch headlong violence to the deftruction of every principle which he had hitherto pretended to revere?

There are, it is true, perfons who have at all times regarded Mr. *Burke* as a fplendid inftance of the depravity of genius—as a man of bafe and time-ferving difpofition, whofe patriotifm was the mere purchafed property of a party, which held him in dependance by the loans granted to him by the Marquis of *Rockingham*; and it was, therefore, thought confiftent enough, when his patron, by a laft act of liberality, had cancelled all legal obligation, that he fhould fet himfelf to fale to the oppofite party, and become the furious opponent of every principle he had been hired to defend. I have endeavoured, however, to judge him with greater charity. I have fought for, and thought I had difcovered, a principle that would account for his conduct in a lefs difhonourable way. My folution, it is true, would ftill have left him among the number of thofe deluded men whofe judgments have been per-

verted

verted by a miſtaken ſenſe of private obligation ; but it would not have reduced him to the level of ſordid corruption.

In ſhort, I conceived Mr. *Burke* to have been throughout a Republican of the old Roman ſchool! or, in other words, a high-toned ariſtocrat. And I readily accounted for this twiſt in his under-ſtanding from the patronage which it had been his misfortune to experience. For it is but too natural with us to regard thoſe inſtitutions as every thing, without which we ſhould ourſelves, apparently, have been nothing. It was, there-fore, not extraordinary that Mr. *Burke*, finding himſelf redeemed, by the powerful and generous patronage of the leader of an ariſtocratic party, from the neceſſity of being a *public lecturer* in a provincial univerſity, and tranſplanted to the more genial ſoil of political influence, ſhould think himſelf bound in *gratitude* to exalt that ariſtocracy to which alone he owed his ex-altation.

Upon this ſolution, his conduct, apparently ſo oppoſite, with reſpect to the *American* and *French* revolutions, is perfectly reconcileable. For with pure, genuine, whole-length ariſtocrats, princes and people are alike indifferent: alike obnoxious, when they aſpire to any ſhare of power; and alike acceptable, as the tools and inſtruments of their ambition. But as, in all mixed governments,

their

their power is of a very doubtful and amphibious nature, but little recognized by the avowed maxims and spirit of the constitution, and depending rather upon the influence of their property, and their talent for intrigue, than either the weight of their functions, or real attachment of the people, as circumstances vary they are obliged to vary the fashion of their sentiments and conduct. Their principle and their object is, however, always the same; and always has been so, whether they instigated the people to destroy a *Tarquin,* or created a *Tarquin* to destroy the people*. Law and liberty are alternately in their mouths; but their liberty is the unrestrained licence of monopolizing oppression, and their law the arbitrary exercise of their own discretion. The dignity of the sovereign, and the sovereignty of the people, are alternate stalking horses for their usurpations. As Mr. *Burke* expresses it—" Popularity and " power they regard alike. These are with them " only different means to obtain their object ; " and have no preference over each other in their " minds, but as one or the other may afford a " surer or less certain prospect of arriving at " their end †."

---

* The reader is particularly recommended to peruse with attention the account given by Dionysius of Halicarnassus (B. IV.) of the murder of Servius Tullius, and of the expulsion of the Tarquins.

† Letter, p. 15.

E

Such

Such are the characteristics of inveterate ariftocracy—of the high-toned *optimates* of mixed and
limited governments: a fet of men widely different from the ancient Tories of this country:—more dangerous, I believe, to the peace
and happinefs of fociety; certainly more deftitute of all fupport from rational and confiftent
principle. Such is the party to which the firft
talents, the moft capacious underftandings, perhaps the beft hearts in this nation, have been too
long enflaved! Such is the party to which I ima-
gined Mr. *Burke* to be infeparably wedded.

This fuppofition is countenanced by his whole
political hiftory. This fuppofition is confirmed
by his own account of what he calls his public
fervices; that is to fay, his fervices to this party.
And, upon this fuppofition, his conduct with refpect to the French revolution, is perfectly reconcileable to his conduct refpecting America.

The principle of the two revolutions was,
perhaps, the fame: though this may be contefted,
at leaft, upon very plaufible grounds. Their operation in this country was, however, widely different. Party difputes ran high, it is true, on
both occafions; and the nation was unhappily
divided into the moft inveterate factions. But in
the former inftance, it was the gentry, the optimacy, the ariftocratic intereft, that moved—that
agitated, and conducted every thing; in the
latter,

latter, the great body of the people—the *common mafs*, had the audacity to judge for themfelves, and inquire into the nature of their rights.

Could an inveterate ariftocrat be expe&ted to tolerate this? Was it not to be expe&ted, that perfons of this defcription, (like the ariftocracy of Spain, upon a fimilar occafion) fhould cling to the throne for prote&tion, againft what they regard-ed as the *invafions of Liberty*, and permit themfelves to be degraded and enfiaved, rather than fuffer the people to be free?

Thus did the candid and liberal part of man-kind account for the apparent inconfiftencies of Mr. *Burke*; and, by referring his whole condu&t to the influence of ariftocratic prejudices, exonerate him from the charge of venal apoftacy. But what fhall we fay now? What opinion fhall we form of the prefent work? To what principle fhall we refer the incongruous fentiments it con-tains? Certainly not to that abhorrence of un-controuled prerogative which infpired him with the enthufiafm of oppofition during the American war, and made rebellion for liberty lovely in his eyes ; thefe fentiments were relinquifhed, for the reafons above ftated, at the very dawn of the French revolution. Certainly, not to thofe feel-ings which, during the difcuffion of the *regency bill*, occafioned that exulting, indecent, and un-feeling exclamation—" The Almighty has hurled

E 2   " him

" him from his throne!"—Mr. *Burké* has learned
a very different " ftyle to a gracious benefactor*!"
His Majefty is now "a benevolent prince," who
" fhews an eminent example, in promoting the
" commerce, manufactures, and agriculture of
" his kingdom;" and " who even in his amufe-
" ments is a patriot, and in his hours of leifure an
" improver of his native foil†:"—a pofition, the
truth of which no one will call in queftion. But
is it more true at this time than before the above-
mentioned period? I, for my part, can perceive
no alteration. The benevolence and patriotifm
of the prefent reign has been fteady, uniform, and
confiftent. At leaft, the only important difference
is, that Mr. *Burke* has now a *penfion* from his
" mild and benevolent fovereign;" and that then he
expected a *place* from his fucceffor! Still lefs can .
we refer this extraordinary pamphlet to thofe
ariftocratical principles which offered the only
folution of his former conduct.

" The government of France," fays that great
oracle, Sir *John Mitford*‡, " was totally over-
" thrown in confequence of the total failure of
" the good opinion of the people;" and hence
that profound and fubtile logician thought himfelf entitled to infer, that it muft neceffarily be
high treafon to fhake the foundations of popular

* Letter, &c. p. 10. † Ibid. p. 44. ‡ Trial of T. Hardy.

opinion:

opinion: but if this conclufion were juft, never was fo capital a treafon committed againft the ariftocratic branch of the conftitution, as by the publication of Mr. *Burke*'s pamphlet.

Is the compofition of ariftocracy fuch as Mr. *Burke* reprefents it?—Then is the very inftitution of ariftocracy radically vicious!—Is it " the offal " thrown to jackals in waiting," after " the lion " has fucked the blood*?" and are " innocent " perfons†," and " bodies of unoffending men†" the " prey" upon which both are pampered?—I am afraid thefe premifes would carry us further than Mr. *Burke* and his new friends are yet prepared to go. I am afraid it would be fomething like high treafon, at leaft, under Lord *Grenville*'s new aƈt, to draw the conclufions that inevitably refult from fuch data!!! And yet if fuch pamphlets are put in circulation by the *advocates* and *penfioners* of government, what aƈt of parliament can prevent the confequences?

Mr. *Burke*, an advocate of government! Mr. *Burke*, the champion of ariftocracy! Mr. *Burke*, the political Atlas who fupports with fuch " great zeal," and fuch " fuccefs,"—" thofe old " prejudices which buoy up the ponderous mafs " of nobility, wealth, and titles‡!" Judge for yourfelves, my fellow citizens: but before you

---

* Letter, &c. p. 41.　† Ibid. p. 42.　‡ Ibid. &c. p. 34.

pronounce, too pofitively, read with attention
his eighty pages of virulent abufe againft
" overgrown dukes, who *opprefs the induftry of*
" *humble men*!"*—" who hold large portions of
" wealth" (" the prodigies of profufe donation †")
" without any apparent merit of their own‡!"
and by their " vaft *landed penfions* §" (obtained by
the blackeft crimes of treachery and oppreflion‖)
" fo enormous as not only to outrage œcono-
" my, but even to ftagger credibility ¶,"—
" trample on the mediocrity of laborious indi-
" viduals** !"

But it is not only with the battle-axe of moral
indignation that Mr. *Burke* affails the ariftocracy
of his country. With equal expertnefs, and
equal ardour, he wings the light, keen fhafts of
fatire and ridicule : nay, fo blunt is his fympathy,
and fo exquifite his animofity, that he even
tears it occafionally with the rude hand-faw of
pointlefs fcurrility††. The rage of *Juvenil*, and
the playful levity of *Horace*, are not fufficient; and
Billingfgate and the fhambles are forced into
alliance with the mufes, the claffics, and the
fciences, to fupply him with terms and meta-
phors fufficiently forcible to exprefs the mighty
hatred with which he labours.

---

* Letter, &c. p. 33. † Ibid. p. 39. ‡ Ibid. p. 34.
§ Ibid. p. 38. ‖ Ibid. p. 41, 42, 43, 44, and 46. ¶ Ibid.
p. 37. ** Ibid. p. 39. †† Ibid. p. 37, 68, 69.

Youthful

Youthful intemperance may furnifh fome apology for hafty and indecorous language: but if
grey hairs expect our reverence, they muft pur-
chafe it by difcretion, wifdom, and moderation.
Mr. *Burke*, however, retains, at three-fcore, his
juvenile contempt for thefe cold qualities—
" this well felected rigour!"—this " preventive
" police of morality*!" The hungry lionefs
rufhes not with fo blind a fury upon her prey,
as he upon the victims of his refentment. I am
told that a noble attendant of the bedchamber
(I mean Lord *Winchelfea*) who turned feveral of
his tenants out of their farms, &c. for being
guilty of diftant relationfhip to me, and of having
read my publications, among other things, complained very bitterly of fome paffages in my
" Peripatetic," which he confidered as calculated
to inflame the minds of the common people
againft the opulent and the great. I will not
venture to affirm that there are no expreffions or
fentiments, in that hafty publication, which, upon
mature confideration, might demand fome foften-
ing or apology. But to fay nothing of the much
more popular and " queftionable fhape" in
which Mr. *Burke's pamphlet* comes before the
public, I defy all the lords of the bedchamber

* Letter, &c. p. 34.

put

put together, to find in the work before-mentioned, or in any other of my productions, paſſages of any thing like the inflammatory nature with thoſe in which the " Letter to a Noble Lord" abounds. I have pleaded, it is true, and while I have a tongue or a pen to exerciſe in ſo juſt a cauſe, I will continue to plead, the cauſe of the oppreſſed and injured labourer. I have reproved the un-feeling and faſtidious pride of greatneſs; and offered ſomething in extenuation for the pilfering vices of laborious wretchedneſs. I have even preſumed to hurl back the charge of diſhoneſty upon " mighty lords, and deſcendants from the " looſe amours of kings," who " rob us, by letters " patent, and ſuffer not a coal to blaze in our " grates, nor an action to be brought for the " recovery of a juſt debt, till they have levied " contribution upon us:" But Mr. *Burke* flies at higher quarry. He pounces at once at hereditary property; calls the birds of prey around him, and excites them to the promiſed banquet.

In ſhort, if the dæmon of anarchy wiſhed to reduce the ſocial frame to chaos, what charms more proper could he ſelect for his incantations than the ingredients of this troubled cauldron? Should ſome prophet of pillage and maſſacre in reality ariſe, what more could he wiſh for than ſuch a Koran? what further inſtructions could he give

give to his apoftles and miffionaries than to comment upon the text of *Edmund Burke,* and pufh
his principles to their moft obvious conclufions?

I truft, however—and, in this one refpect, my
opportunities of forming a juft conclufion have
been much fuperior to my antagonift's—I truft,
that what are called the common people of this
country are in no danger of being ftimulated to
fuch exceffes as this letter fometimes pretends to
deprecate, but more frequently appears calculated to provoke. I too have laboured " with
" very great zeal, and I believe with fome degree
" of fuccefs *" (rather more, if I am not miftaken,
than Mr. *Burke* can boaft of in his attempt to
" fupport old prejudices *") not indeed " to
" difcountenance enquiry *" but to give it a juft
direction;—to point out to the poorer fort in
particular of my fellow citizens, fmarting and
writhing under the lafh of oppreffion and con-
tumely, the peaceful means of redrefs; to fhew
them the diftinction between tumult and reform
—between the amelioration and the diffolution
of fociety—the removal of oppreffion, and the
fanguinary purfuits of pillage and revenge. I
truft that the falutary leffon has not been en-
forced in vain—that *whatever calamities may refult
to fociety, from the prefent enormous inequality in the*

* Letter, &c. p. 34.

F   *diftribution*

*diftribution of property, all tumultuary attacks upon
individual poffeffion, all attempts, or pretences of level-
ling and equalization, muft be attended with maffacres
and affaffinations, equally deftructive to the fecurity of
every order of mankind; and, after a long ftruggle of
afflictions and horrors, muft terminate at laft, not in
equalization, but in a moft iniquitous transfer, by which
cut-throats and affaffins would be enabled to found a
new order of nobility, more infufferable, becaufe more
ignorant and ferocious, than thofe whom their daggers
had fupplanted.*

The friends of liberty know that, fooner or
later, the progrefs of reafon muft produce (perhaps, at no diftant period) an effential reformation
in the government and inftitutions of this country: but (unlefs the frantic and defperate councils
of fuch men as Mr. *Burke* and Mr. *Windham,*
fhould unhinge all fociety, *under pretence of preferv-
ing order)* no part of the exceffes which have
rent and convulfed the devoted land of *France*
need be dreaded in *England:* for the caufes of
thofe exceffes do not exift among us. Reform,
like a long-woo'd virgin, fhall come at laft, in
the unfullied robes of Peace, and, in the Temple
of Concord, fhall give her hand to Reafon. But
fuch hymeneals fuit not the taftes and difpofitions of Mr. *Burke;* for placemen and penfioners
will not be invited to the banquet. The mar-
riage of Tyranny and Corruption, in a robe of
blood,

blood, would be more in harmony with his difor-
dered and irritated imagination; with a legion of
foreign mercenaries to protect the pomp, and a
proceffion of Inquifitors, and an *Auto da Fé*, to
clofe the accuftomed revels!

Such, at leaft, are the only orgies, for which the
vows and the offerings of Mr. *Burke* are calculated to prepare. Such alone are the fyftems to
which his maxims and fentiments are reconcileable: For if, on one hand, all democratic innova-
tion—all reform is to be pertinacioufly refifted,
and on the other, all refpect for rank, fortune, and
hereditary ftation are to be torn away, by the
impaffioned hand of perfonal rancour and factious
malevolence—if the people, deprived of all legal
weight and influence in the legiflature of the
country, and therefore of all attachment from
rational and well-placed affection, are to be
ftimulated to perfonal hatred and animofity
againft the noble, the wealthy, and the great,
whom they are to be taught by *miniflerial hirelings*
(oh! that fuch a mind fhould ever be included in
fuch a defcription!) to regard as the plunderers
of their anceftors, and the oppreffors of themfelves,
what but tyranny the moft unqualified—what but
blood—what but foreign mercenaries, and the
united horrors of inquifitorial and military defpotifm, can long fuftain that rule which minifters
pretend to be fo anxious to preferve unaltered?

What

What *but* this?—Nay: *not this, nor more!!!*—
Britons may be led: but driven they will not be.
They have fpirit—they have intelligence—they
have a manly firmnefs—they have fome knowledge of their rights, and a keen defire to poffefs
them. In fhort, they are men who live towards the clofe of the eighteenth century, and
have feen two Revolutions: and if Bifhops continue to preach, that " they have nothing to do
" with the laws but to obey them;" and Lord
Chancellors to declare, that " the laws they are
" to obey ought to be couched in fuch terms
" that they cannot comprehend them!"—If
wafteful wars are to create famines, and illuftrious
peers are to confole the half-ftarved people with
the reflection, that " their fcanty mefs would
" have been ftill more fcanty, if fo many of
" their friends and relatives had not been
" flaughtered;" or, as Mr. *Windham* would call
it, *killed off*, " in foreign expeditions!"—If every
door is to be clofed againft peaceful remonftrance
and complaint, and Secretaries at War are to
thruft obnoxious ftatutes down our throats with
the fabres of armed affociators!—and if, finally,
every gallant patriot, noble or fimple, who has
the generofity to ftem the torrent of corruption,
is to be befet by treafury blood hounds, and
hunted with threats of confifcation and profcription:

tion: by the great terror that fwells my heart, as imagination conjures up the picture, I do not believe that earth or hell have power to fuftain the fyftem; but that which *France* has been, *Britain* too foon muft be!

If fuch events fhould take place, whom has the country to thank but the *Grenvilles*, the *Weft-morelands*—the *Pitts*, and *Windhams?*—If property fhould be fhaken, and nobility go to wreck, who founds the Indian yell of pillage and defolation, but the Right Honourable *Edmund Burke,* with his " Letter to a noble Lord?"

In vain fhall the advocates of this political maniac accufe me of mifreprefenting his arguments, by generalizing obfervations which he has confined to a particular inftance. I do no more than every reader of his pamphlet muft inevitably do. It is the Duke of *Bedford,* indeed, that is oftenfibly attacked; but the whole body of nobility and landed proprietors, are wounded through his fide. Let not the partizans of the minifter weakly and wickedly fuppofe, " the " rival honours of the houfe of *Ruffel* are " blighted by this pamphlet, and public odium " excited againft their wide poffeffions; but we " have yet—

" Golden opinions from all ranks of men,
" Which may be worn ftill in their neweft glofs."
SHAKESPEARE.

Let

Let them not, I fay, " lay this flattering
" unction to their fouls." There is not one argument of moral reprehenfion—one ftroke of fatire,
or ridicule—one intemperate expreffion of de-
gradation or abufe, that does not equally apply
to them all. Old nobility and new, all are included—all are alike the victims of Mr. *Burke's*
irritated pride and immeafurable refentments.
Their patents, their deeds of gift, their titles,
and their rent-rolls, all—all are confumed together in this conflagration of his inflamed and all-
inflaming mind!

If the eftates of the Duke of *Bedford* deferve
the odious appellation of " landed penfions *,"
are not the eftates of the Dukes of *Portland*, of
Rutland, of *Richmond*, of the Earls of *Weftmore-
land*, *Winchelfea*, *Lonfdale*, and the long train of
et ceteras, " landed penfions" alfo? Is the Duke
of *Bedford* a " Leviathan among the creatures
" of the crown, who plays and frolics in the
" ocean of royal bounty," (by which, I fuppofe,
we are to underftand that the king, whenever
his virtuous and difinterefted minifters fhall fo
advife, may withdraw his *bounty*†, and transfer
thefe " landed penfions," to more *grateful* fer-
vants!) is not the Earl *Fitzwilliam* a " Leviathan"
alfo? and, would not all the difgufting details

---

* Letter, &c. p. 38.   † If this is not the meaning of
this language, what does it mean?

of

of this figure, in which Mr. *Burke* indulges his imagination, equally apply in one inſtance as in the other? Does he not, alſo, " lay floating " many a rood *?" And if the " overgrown" bulk of the one " oppreſſes the induſtry of humble " men †," are not the unwieldy proportions of the other equally oppreſſive? Was Mr. *Ruſſel*, in the time of *Henry* the eighth, a " *Jackall* in wait- " ing ‡?" What are the *Hawkeſburies*, the *Lough- boroughs*, the *Macdonalds*, and the long liſt of new-created peers, whoſe wholeſale elevation has tended, not a little, to ſhake the preſcriptive reverence, or in Mr. *Burke's* own words, " thoſe " old prejudices §," which can alone ſupport a houſe of *hereditary legiſlators?* If it is a diſ-grace to the Duke of *Bedford* to have been " ſwaddled and rocked, and dandled into a " legiſlator ‖," have not the whole body of nobility, by deſcent, become legiſlators in the ſame ridiculous manner?—If I were not afraid of being ſuſpeЄted of courting the favour of party, (than which nothing, I believe, is more deſtruЄive to the energies of genuine patriotiſm) or bowing to the ſplendour of wealth and pa-tronage (than which nothing is more degrading to the free-born mind!) it would be only a tri-bute of juſtice, to the value and ability of late

* Letter, &c. p. 37. † Ibid, p. 33. ‡ Ibid, p. 41.
§ Ibid, p. 34. ‖ Ibid, p. 28.

exertions

exertions to fay, that it would be well for the country, and for the honour of that houfe, of which the Duke of *Bedford* has *rendered himfelf* a *diftinguifhed ornament*—if this legiflative *fwaddling*, and *rocking*, and *dandling*, had been uniformly as efficient to the end propofed. On the contrary, how many of our illuftrious nobles (aye, and of thofe whom Mr. *Burke* muft now rank among the number of his friends!) are no better, to this day, than " mewling in a nurfe's arms;" or, what is worfe, with a criminal fupinenefs, equally difhonourable to their rank and to their nature, are abandoning every thing to the fpoil and ufurpations of a fet of jobbers, loan contractors, Change-alley calculators and adventurers, who have no other claim to the implicit confidence they enjoy, than what is derived from the difgrace and mifery, the ruin, defolation and famine, which their mad projects, and defperate fpeculations have brought upon the country—and, indeed, upon the whole of Europe?

But this is not the only inftance in which the flail of Mr. *Burke* ftrikes harder behind than it does before. I do not trouble myfelf to enquire whether this firft leaf of " *Burke's new Peerage,*" afford a fpecimen of accuracy and impartiality, or of mifreprefentation and malevolence. The queftion with me (and the only queftion of real importance to fociety) is, not how property was
acquired

acquired three hundred years ago? but—how it is now employed? If the Duke of *Bedford* is difpofed, as I hope and truft he is, to employ his great property and influence to the protection of the liberties and happinefs of his country, the people will have an intereft in the protection of that property. If there be others who are difpofed to abufe their advantages, to the flavery and deftruction of mankind, let them beware, left they urge the people to do that in *felf-defence*, which, from principle, they would abhor: for it is not very ftrange that grinding oppreffion fhould fometimes force the haraffed multitude to reflect, that the rights and happinefs of millions are of more importance than the fecurity and poffeffions of a few. The alternative, it is true, is dreadful: but the crime is with thofe who compel a nation to choofe between fuch hideous extremes.

Regarding property in this point of view, I enquire not how " the firft Earl of *Bedford* " acquired the vaft eftates which he has tranfmitted to his pofterity; nor by what title *John a Gaunt* held thofe immenfe *commons*, which he bequeathed *in perpetuum* to the poor of the refpective diftricts. I would not even be very curious to enquire into the means by which the wretched peafantry have been deprived of thefe freeholds, and their eftates transferred to a few

G   wealthy

wealthy proprietors; unlefs it were with a view
of preventing future encroachments. But, furely,
Mr. *Burke* does not fuppofe us ignorant enough
to believe, that Mr. *Ruffel* is the only founder of a
family, whofe merits it would be painful to
probe. Does he call us to look back to the
reign of *Henry* the eighth?—who, by the way,
tyrant and monfter as he was, (and even Mr.
Burke, it feems, is aware that kings can fometimes be fuch) by exterminating from the
country thofe lazy and peftiferous drones, the
monks and religionifts " of his time and coun-
" try *," made an ample atonement to fociety for
all his crimes!—Does Mr. *Burke*, I fay, call upon
us to look back to the reign of this eighth
Harry? Let this " *defender* of the high and emi-
" nent †" reflect, that we can look further! or we
need not look fo far! Let him afk the houfe of
Bentinck, whether there were no " prodigies of
" profufe donation" in the time of *William* the
third? Whether the " lions" of the houfe of *Naffau*
had not their " jackalls," as well as thofe of the
houfe of *Tudor?* Let him afk the proudeft he
that ever traced his genealogy to the times of
the Norman robber, whether there were no inftances, even in *thofe good old days*, of " immo-
" derate grants taken from the recent confifcation

* Letter, &c. p. 43.   † Ibid. p. 42.

" of

" of the ancient nobility of the land * ?" Had
none of the landed penfions of that day their
" fund in the murder of innocent perfons, or in
" the pillage of bodies of men †," more truly
" unoffending" than thofe cloiftered drones and
juggling vifionaries, whofe difperfion Mr. *Burke* fo
pathetically bewails?

Could the monks of *Wooburn* and *Taviftock*, and
the murdered franklins and freeholders of thofe
days of old, rife at once from their graves, (like
the furies who purfued *Oreftes)* to harafs the prefent poffeffors of their refpective feats, whofe
wrongs would found moft terrible in the affrighted
ears of nobility?—whofe appeal would be moft
forcible to retributive juftice?

Mr. *Burke* has done an irreparable injury to
the caufe of ariftocracy by provoking this difcuffion ; and, if an antidote is not applied, which I
truft it will, by fair and manly expofition of the
fubject, has fet a poifon in circulation moft dangerous to the health and exiftence of the focial frame.

The attachment, however, of this polemic to
ariftocracy, appears at leaft to be as fincere as his
religion. He pretends to fofter and protect the
former, and he tears it up by the roots, from that
only foil in which any inftitution can flourifh—
the opinions of the people over whom it fpreads.

* Letter, &c. p. 41.   † Ibid. 42.

He

He pretends to be a zealot in behalf of the latter, and he acts on the direct converse of the
position upon which the morality of that syftem
is profeffedly built. The decalogue only de-
nounces vengeance upon the pofterity of offenders
to the *third and fourth generations*; but promifes
mercy to thoufands of the righteous and good.
Mr. *Burke*, on the contrary, vifits the fins of the
forefathers upon generations without end, and
paffes by their virtues, as of no account at all.

I repeat it—for I am no fimulator; nor have
the popular fchools in which I have been fafhioned, (whatever contempt Mr. *Burke* may *now* think
fit to entertain for them) made me fo keen a
difputant, as to be willing, for the fake of victory,
to appear the thing I am not. I repeat it, therefore, I do not ftand up as the advocate of hereditary diftinctions, or hereditary honours. All
honour, and all fhame, are, in my calculation,
merely perfonal. Goods and chattels may be
heritable property; and in fuch a fociety as we
are members of, I am convinced that it is neceffary they fhould be fo. But moral and intellectual
diftinctions, (the fountains of all real honour) are
neither heritable nor transferable; nor is it in the
power of human laws to make them fuch. They
begin and they end with the immediate poffeffor.
I admit, at the fame time, that anceftral reputation fometimes operates very powerfully in the
way

way of example. Strong inftances of this are to
be found both in the hiftory of the ancient and
the modern world: and if the Duke of *Bedford*
has been roufed to his late exertions by a proud
admiration of the conduct of that anceftor who,
in the infamous reign of Charles the fecond,
fealed his attachment to the principles of liberty
with his blood, I rejoice that he had fuch an example to fet before his eyes; nor is it juftice to
fociety to fuffer that example to be forgotten. If
his Grace, in defiance of Mr. *Burke*'s admonition*,
fhould ever condefcend to attend my lecture,
(where I have fometimes been honoured with the
plaudits of as fine fcholars, as diftinguifhed patriots, and almoft as exalted geniufes as my ca-
lumniating antagonift) I would endeavour, it is
true, to convince him that there is a furer and a
better motive of virtuous action: that the love of
mankind is better than the pride of anceftry:
that it is more noble to enquire how nations and
generations can be moft effectually ferved, than
what our forefathers did, or what they would
have done: and that to be what we ought, is
to be fomething more than the moft virtuous
anceftor has ever been! But if mankind are ftill
to be eftimated, not by individuals, but by families
—if the whole race is to be regarded as a body cor-
porate, and the living reprefentative to be account-

---

* Letter, &c. p. 35.

able

able for the actions of the whole, still let us pay some little regard to justice—let us balance fairly the debtor and the creditor, and set down the good as well as the bad.

If this is the way in which we are to proceed, the house of *Ruffel* has nothing to dread in the settlement of the long account. Let Mr. *Burke* paint the first Earl of *Bedford* in the blackest colours his imagination can supply—let all that he has afferted pass unqueftioned, and more, if more can be found, be added to the account; the virtuous refolution of Lord *William Ruffel*, who, in the full poffeffion of all that youth, and rank, and wealth, paternal pride, and conjugal affection could beftow, difdained to preferve his life by fhrinking from his principles, is an ample atonement for all.

But it is not ftrange that Mr. *Burke* fhould be blind, not only to juftice, but to the interefts alfo of the order he profeffes to defend; for what fo blind as the headlong fury of felfifh and irritable pride? What fo precipitate as the paffions and refentments of a mind evidently and avowedly uncontrouled by any curb of principle?—which, regardlefs of the unity and immutability of truth, profeffes to fubmit its calculations and conclufions to the fluctuating decifions of intereft, favour, or averfion—and on queftions that relate to " the " theory [and practice] of moral proportions *,"

* Letter, &c. p. 9.

to

to ufe " one ftyle to a gracious benefactor; ano-
" ther to a proud and infulting foe*?"

That fuch were the motives and caufes that
produced this pamphlet, the pamphlet itfelf has
put beyond all queftion and difpute. " Why
" will his Grace," it is faid, " *by attacking me*, force
" me reluctantly to compare my little merit with
" that which obtained from the crown thofe pro-
" digies of profufe donation,† " &c. " Let him
" remit his rigor on the difproportion between
" merit and reward in others, and they will make
" no enquiry into the origin of his fortune‡!"

Was ever rectitude of mind more publicly dif-
avowed than in this fentence? Was ever felf-
love and refentment fo openly proclaimed paramount to all principle? Either the enquiry is
right, and ought to require no inducement from
perfonal motives; or it is wrong, and no perfonal
motive ought to provoke it. But this, I fuppofe,
is the *gratitude* about which Mr. *Burke* makes
fo much parade:—" You do injuftice to man-
" kind, that I may reap the benefit of it; and
" I will do the like injuftice, that the benefit may
" be reaped by you!"

Such is the *common traffic of gratitude and private
obligation!* Such, according to " the *old* fect
" in politics and morals," is the fquare rule of
virtue!

* Letter, &c. p. 10. † Ibid. p. 39. ‡ Ibid. p. 47.

This

This fentiment is ftill more nakedly expreffed in another place. " *Had he permitted me* " *to remain in quiet*, I fhould have faid 'tis his " eftate; that's enough. It is his by law; what " have I to do with its hiftory? He would na- " turally have faid on his fide, 'tis this man's " fortune.—He is as good now, as my anceftor " was two hundred and fifty years ago. I am *a* " *young man with very old penfions*; *he is an old man* " *with very young penfions,—that's all*!*"

What is this but faying, in other words, that men of eftate and property, and the nobles of the land in particular—the *hereditary guardians of the rights and properties of the people*, are bound in good policy to countenance all the growing peculations of corruption; and, if they refufe to do fo, that the *new peculators* will turn round upon the *old proprietors* with all the fury of a dangerous and defperate revenge, fhake the foundations of their property, and endeavour to excite againft them all the popular odium that may lead to pillage and tumult! But if thefe paffages reveal the *felfifh irritability* and *lax morality* of the writer, what fhall we fay to the fentiment expofed in the enfuing?—" Since the total body of my " fervices have obtained the acceptance of my " fovereign, it would be abfurd in me to range

---

* Letter, &c. p. 39.

" my felf

" myfelf on the fide of the Duke of *Bedford* and
" the *London Correfponding Society*!*"

What, then—are we to underftand that if *the
total body of his fervices* had not been accepted,
that is to fay, rewarded by the *animating foul of a
good penfion*, he would have ranged himfelf on
the fide of the Duke of *Bedford* and the London
Correfponding Society?—In other words, are we
to underftand that his hoftility to liberty, and
the negociation for his penfion, began at the
fame time?

For the honour of human genius, I would fain
hope, in defiance of fo many concurring circumftances, and of Mr. *Burke's* own teftimony, that
this is not entirely a correct ftatement of the
cafe, and that it is yet poffible to find fome way
of accounting for his conduct, without referring
every thing to confcious and voluntary corruption.
Be this, however, as it may—I truft that the
public are not at any lofs to decide which of the
important fervices, fo oftentatioufly difplayed in
this fplendid farrago of abufe and egotifm, it was
that occafioned that " *able, vigorous, and well-in-*
" *formed ftatefman*†, Lord *Grenville*, to have the
" goodnefs and condefcenfion" both " to fay"
and do fuch " *handfome things* in his behalf ‡." I
will not enter into the perfonal merits or de-

---

* Letter, &c. p. 59.   † Ibid. p. 3.   ‡ Ibid. p. 2.

H   merits

merits of Mr. *Burke*, nor into the general ques-
tion of the propriety or impropriety of his penfion. I leave this enquiry in the hands of older
and of better judges. Mr. *Burke* would, of
courfe, object to my " being on the inqueft of his
" *quantum meruit* * "—(may his fate never be in the
hand of a lefs candid juror!) He, of courfe,
" cannot recognize in my few" (he cannot, however, add my " *idle*) years, the competence to judge
" of his long and laborious life*;" and I am
certainly as well attached, as he, at this time, finds
it convenient to be, " not only to the letter, but
" to the fpirit of the old Englifh law of trial by
" peers†;" and fhould be forry either to prejudge
him by a *garbelled and inflammatory report*, fabri-
cated in the guilt-concealing cave of *fecrecy*, to
prefent him with a packed jury, or to traverfe
his challenges. But Mr. *Burke* will not himfelf
deny that from " the total body of his fervices," it
is eafy to fingle forth the limb or feature whofe
grace and attraction won the rich prize of royal—
or rather of minifterial favour. Mr. *Burke* himfelf
will not pretend to doubt that, great and important
as thofe fervices might be, which he has fo well
enumerated, his " unexampled toil in the fervice
" of his country‡," his " œconomical reforms§,"
his " ftudies of political œconomy," which he had

---

* Letter, &c. p. 9. † Ibid. p. 8. ‡ Ibid. p. 6.
§ Ibid. p. 18.

purfued

purfued " from his very early youth," and by
which " the houfe" [of commons] " has profitted"
fo much, " for above eight and twenty years*,"
together with all that " preparation and difcipline
" to political warfare," by which he " had earned
" his penfion before he fet his foot in Saint Ste-
" phen's chapel†," all, all would have been neglected and forgotten, but for his conduct with
refpect to the French Revolution. All that he
" did, and all that he prevented from being
" done‡," even at that time (1780), when "wild
" and favage infurrection quitted the woods, and
" prowled about the ftreets in the name of re-
" form§," and " a fort of national convention" (of
which his new friend Mr. *Pitt* now, perhaps, *re-
collects* that he was a member) "nofing parliament
" in the very feat of its authority‖," threatened
England " with the honour of leading up the
" death-dance of democratic revolution! ¶" all,
all would have lain in thanklefs oblivion—even
the *eternal impeachment*, " on which (of all his fer-
" vices) he values himfelf the moft**," would
have failed to influence " minifters to confider
" his fituation††," if it had not been for the
zeal and ardour with which he founded the
trumpet of alarm againft the *ideal danger* of

* Letter, &c. p. 28.   † Ibid. p. 27.   ‡ Ibid. p. 23.
§ Ibid. p. 13. ‖ Ibid. p. 14. ¶ Ibid. p. 13. ** Ibid. p. 27.
†† Ibid. p. 6.

" rude

" rude inroads of *Gallic tumult* * ," called up, with his hideous yells, the hell-born fiend of political perfecution, and, turning the houfe of commons into a mountebank's ftage, dagger-ftruck every imagination, and plunged his country —plunged all Europe, into the moft frantic, the moft terrible, the moft defolating war, that ever fcourged the univerfe!

This was the crown of all his labours—" the " Corinthian capital," that gave the finifhing grace to the temple of public utility his life had been fpent in rearing. But for this " the four and " a half per cents had been kept full in his eye †" " in vain. He might have enjoyed, it is true, in vifta, the profpect of this trophy of " the œcono-" my of felection and proportion ‡," but never would he have beheld the minifter entering the porch to confecrate the fpoils and offerings at his fhrine.

If I were not impatient to enter into more important matter, and unwilling to extend too far the limits of this pamphlet, I would fain make fome few animadverfions upon thefe four and a half per cents. I would fain enquire into the grounds of that exultation with which Mr. *Burke* compares the funds and fources of his penfion, with thofe that adminiftered to the exaltation of the houfe of Ruffel. I would fain enquire whether

* Letter, &c. p. 54.   † Ibid. p. 25.   ‡ Ibid. 33.

it

it be more vicious to enrich oneſelf with the plunder of *dormitories*, and by the extermination of ſlothful, juggling, monks (who, like devouring *locuſts*, prey on the green leaf of uſeful induſtry, and blight its hopeful fruitage in the bud) or *even* with the confiſcations of attainted nobles, the deſcendants, according to Mr. *Burke*, of former " jackalls in waiting"—for the argument holds equally true *ad infinitum*; or to draw the means of luxury and profuſion from taxes extorted from the hard-earned pittance of the labourer, and thereby to make the ſpare meal of poverty ſtill more ſcanty and comfortleſs. Mr. *Burke* has quibbles and ſophiſtries, and his friend, Mr. *Windham*, has metaphyſical ſubtilities, I make no doubt, to repel this charge; but if I had time to puſh the queſtion home, I could prove, by calculations as incontrovertible as any in the miniſter's arithmetic, that every penſion that rewards the baſeneſs of political apoſtacy, ſtrips the wretched family of the peaſant and the manufacturer of a portion of their ſcanty bread.

Mr. *Burke* may therefore congratulate himſelf, as much as he pleaſes, upon the " ſpontaneous " bounty" of " the Royal Donor," and " the " goodneſs and condeſcenſion" of " his miniſ-" ters*;" but his penſion is, in reality, a beggar's

* Letter, &c. p. 6 and 2.

cap,

cap, thrown by the way fide, to receive the
farthing of the pooreft paffenger; while, to ag-
gravate the difgrace, taxation, like the crippled
foldier in *Gil Blas*, refts its blunderbufs upon the
ftile, and converts the pretended "charity *" into
an act of plunder.

But my pamphlet is fwelling beyond its intended proportion; and I muft haften to more .
important matter. I leave, therefore, all confideration of the general merits of the penfioner, all
comparifon of the proportion between the fervices and the reward; and all enquiry into the
operation of the penfion, that I may examine the
particular conduct without which all his other
fervices would have been of no avail; and canvas
the principles upon which that conduct was profeffedly built.

"If I am unworthy," fays the pamphlet, "the mi-
" nifters are worfe than prodigal †:" and if with refpect to *French affairs* his conduct has been inconfiftent with juftice, policy, and the fecurity and happinefs of mankind, the greater his former fervices,
the more criminal thofe minifters muft appear:
for the fyftem indeed muft be rotten to the core,
when a life of honourable fervice can only obtain
its reward by an old age of depredation and
mifchief.

* Letter, &c. p. 33.   † Ibid. p. 7.

Mr.

Mr. *Burke*, it is true, modeftly declines "the high "diftinction," and "the glory" of being confidered as the exclufive " author of the war*;" and as I am not at all defirous of removing *refponfibility* from the fhoulders where the conftitution has placed it, I am ready to exonerate him from the charge. I believe that the minifters of this country had refolved, from the firft dawn of the *Revolution in France*, to feize the earlieft opportunity of attacking that nation. I believe, that but for the minifters of this country, the profligate and fatal treaty of *Pilnitz* never would have been figned; *France* and the Empire would not have been embroiled in war; the exceffes which have difgraced the greateft and moft glorious event in the annals of mankind, would never have been perpetrated ; and that *Louis* XVI. might, perhaps, to this day have continued " King of the French." I believe, alfo, that if no fuch man as Mr. *Burke* had been in exiftence, Mr. *Pitt*—or more properly fpeaking, Lord *Hawkefbury*, would neverthelefs have plunged us into this unhappy conteft. Mr. *Burke* and his *dagger* were therefore only inftruments (powerful inftruments, however,) in exciting that terror and alarm, which gave, among certain claffes at leaft, a degree of popularity to the meafure, without which the minifter would

---

* Letter, &c. p. 79.

have found it difficult to fulfil *his continental en-gagements!*

It was Mr. *Burke* who affifted him, in this em-barraffment, by founding the *tocfin* of alarm, and creating a real danger by proclaiming one that was imaginary. It was Mr. *Burke* who made himfelf cryer to the new inquifition, and pre-pared the way for the *Reevefes*, the *Devaynefes*, and the *Idefons*, whofe *departmental Star Chambers*, and *Revolutionary Committees**, have polluted the ftream of adminiftrative juftice, and debafed the character of the nation. He it was that, like a political dog-ftar, fhook " from his horrid hair" diftemper and delirium; till the brain-fever of property maddened the whole land; and great bankers and wealthy merchants, furrounded by their clerks and dependants, (the myrmidons of the ware-room and counting-houfe) turned

---

* This phrafe may found rather harfhly in the ears of *loyal affociators!* but it fhould be remembered, that there are revo-lutions againft liberty, as well as revolutions for it: revolutions made by governors againft the people, as well as revolutions made by the people againft the government. The latter of thefe have always, I believe, proceeded from neceffity; been actuated, in the firft inftance, by right principles; and been productive of ultimate good. The former have as uniformly refulted from the ambition, rapacity, and tyranny of wicked counfellors, and have been productive of oppreffion and mife-ry, and generally of *ultimate revolt!* Thefe revolutions are, in reality, the caufes, and the juftifications of the other.—But of this more in the text.

Merchant

Merchant Taylor's Hall into a bear garden ; put
Billingfgate and Bedlam to the bluſh by their
diſgraceful, and outrageous conduct; and thus
preſented us with a modern illuſtration of that
profound and indubitable remark of *Machiavel,*
that " tumults and diſturbances are more
" frequently created by the wealthy and power-
" ful, than by the poorer claſſes of ſociety*."

In

---

* See that invaluable work " Diſcourſes on the firſt
" decade of Titus Livius." Verſions of this neglected book,
both in *French* and in *Engliſh*, are to be met with upon almoſt
every ſtall: and my readers cannot do better than tranſplant
it, and, indeed, the whole of this author's works, into their
libraries. The doctrine above quoted, will be found at ſome
length in book i. c. 5.

Some, perhaps, may think that I have treated this " re-
" ſpectable body of men !" rather too harſhly in this paſſage:
but the turbulent yells, the grinning diſtortions of im-
paſſioned countenance, the joſtlings, and perſonal violence,
with which every individual was aſſailed who attempted to
oppoſe their reſolutions, cannot but live in the memory of
all who were preſent at that meeting. The outrageous and
aſſaſſin-like attack made by a part of this *reſpectable body*
upon Mr. *Favel,* as he was departing from the hall, fixes a
ſtain of a deeper dye, and would furniſh ſome colour, at leaſt,
to the arguments of thoſe who might wiſh to perſuade us, that
the boaſted police of this country, is not ſo much intended
to preſerve the peace, and protect the perſons of the people,
as to enforce a blind and abject ſubmiſſion to the will of the
governing party! The conduct of theſe ſame *reſpectable
gentlemen* at Grocer's Hall was, I underſtand, ſtill more outrageous. Let any perſon compare theſe facts with the tran-

quil,

I

In fhort, it was Mr. *Burke* who condefcended to be the "jackal," not of a *lion*, but of an *ape*, who, having run through all the tricks and metamor-phofes of apoftacy, determined, at laft, to become a beaft of prey, though he had neither the courage, nor the fagacity, to ftart his own game.

His new ally, however, caught up the fcent with all imaginable keennefs. No fooner did the troubles in France make their appearance, than he began to beat the war-provoking hide of " old *John Zifca**," and call out for carnage and blood.—Like *Collins*'s perfonification of Anger, forth

> " ———— he rufhed : his eyes on fire
> " In lightnings own his fecret ftings!"

and, this too, at a time when every thing in that country was going on fo humanely, fo philofo-phically, fo benevolently, that every generous heart in Europe fympathifed with the triumphs

---

quil, firm, and orderly proceedings of the immenfe multitudes of *common people* affembled at *Chalk Farm*, *Copenhagen Houfe*, and *Mary-le-bone Fields*—the regularity with which they tranf-acted their bufinefs, and the peaceable manner in which they difperfed, as foon as it was over; let them add to this, an atten-tive examination of the behaviour of the plebeians and of the patrician order, in what are called the *feditions* of ancient *Rome*, and then let them draw what arguments they can in favour of the maxims and fyftem of the prefent admini-ftration.

* Letter, &c p. 3.

of Gallic liberty; and mankind began to lofe
their nationality, and nobles their prejudices, in
the unbounded admiration of an event that pro-
mifed a fpeedy extinction of thofe fyftems of
devaftation and ambition, which have hitherto
been the greateft fcourges of the univerfe.

It is in vain that Mr. *Burke* now raves about
maffacres, and fanguinary executions. It is in
vain, that he difgufts our imaginations with tedious rhapfodies about " foul and ravenous birds
" of prey----obfcene revolutionary harpies, fprung
" from night and hell, or from that chaotic
" anarchy which generates equivocally all
" monftrous, all prodigious things * !" At the
time when his firft wild and frantic publication on this fubject miniftered to the infidious
defigns of his prefent patrons, no exceffes
had taken place which could juftify his abufe,
or afford the leaft colour for regarding the
French revolutionifts as maniacs " who thought
" *The whole duty of man* confifted in deftruction †."
The revolution was then in the hands of " philo-
" fophers," and " literary men ‡ !" It had not yet
fallen (as afterwards, from the unprincipled interference of foreign defpots, and the ftill more
fatal influence of *foreign gold*, fcattered among
emiffaries " in the night cellars of *Paris*," to

* Letter, &c. p. 21.   † Ibid. p. 57.   ‡ Ibid. p. 57.

hire

hire intrigue, and provoke infurrection, it did moft undoubtedly fall) under the management of " bravoes and banditti"----of " robbers and " affaffins." If his declamations againft the changes that have taken place in that country, had never been heard till the fyftem " of pillage, " oppreffion, *arbitrary imprifonment*, confifcation, " exile, revolutionary judgment, and *legalized* " *premeditated murder**," had been adopted; and thofe declamations had been abandoned when the cruelty and wickednefs of this fyftem were relinquifhed, he might have claimed fome credit, perhaps, for his humanity; and have laid lefs open to the fufpicion of a grounded abhorrence to every principle of liberty. Even then, however, we muft have pitied the confufion of intellect that could not feparate principles from unprincipled actions; and continue to revere the fentiments of truth and juftice, however they might be violated by their profeffors: or rather by individuals of the country in which they were profeffed.

But it is the profeffion and occupation of this fingular writer, to confound all diftinctions by affected *antithefis*; to deftroy all unities of time, place, and action, for the purpofes of mifreprefentation; to bewilder the underftandings of his

* Letter, &c. p. 64.

readers

readers by incongruous mixtures of fact and fiction, and to build his conclusions upon artful transpositions, that unite things together which have no connection, and make causes the consequences of their own effects. His mode of analysis is to break down the whole series of events into one chaotic mass; and then, selecting such parts as are best suited to his purpose, and arranging them according to his own arbitrary fancy, to draw conclusions that contradict all the facts of history, and all the dictates of unsophisticated reason. Thus, for example, the French Revolution having at different periods, and under different circumstances, brought into action, upon the political theatre, some of the most enlightened philosophers that ever adorned, and some of the fiercest cannibals that have disgraced, the modern world, Mr. *Burke*, that every thing French, and every thing revolutionary, may be brought into abhorrence at once, confounds the two classes together under the denomination " of the Cannibal Philosophers of France *;" and exclaims, with affected astonishment, " In the French Revolution every thing is " new; and from want of preparation to meet so " unlooked for an evil, every thing is dangerous. " Never, before this time, was a set of literary " men converted into a gang of robbers and

* Letter, &c. p. 56, 59.

" assassins.

" affaffins. Never before, did a den of bravoes
" and banditti, affume the garb and tone of an
" academy of philofophers *."

Never before! No, nor now. The author of
" Reflections on the French Revolution," and
the author of the " Rights of Man," are not more
diftinct—the fentiments of *Edmund Burke* on the
American war, and the fentiments of *Edmund
Burke* on the prefent crufade, are not more oppofite than the men and the motives he has thus
confounded together. They were men, not only
diftinct, but in pofitive oppofition. As well
might the till late unheard-of maxims of defpotifm, faid to have been delivered by the Bifhop
of *Rochefter* and Lord *Loughborough*, be attributed
by future hiftorians to the Earl of *Lauderdale*,
by whom they were fo fpiritedly and fo properly
expofed†!—as well might *Thomas Paine* be re-
proached with the virulent and unprincipled
malignancy of ftigmatifing the oppreffed, laborious, and moft valuable claffes of fociety as
a " fwinifh multitude," becaufe he lived and
wrote in the fame age with the being who out-
raged humanity with fuch fcurrility, as the
crimes of *Robefpierre*, of *Couthon*, and of *Marat*,
of the ATTORNEY GENERAL *Fouquiere*, and the
hangman *Le Bone*, be charged to the account of

* Letter, &c. p. 57.
† Debates on Lord *Grenville's* new treafon bill.

the

the *Condorcets*, the *Isnards*, the *Rochefoucaults*, and the *Rolands*, who were the *victims*, not the *authors*, of the crimes which we deplore.

That the philosophers of France were too cold, too speculative, too slow and cautious, to have saved their country, in the desperate condition into which they were plunged by the coalition of German despots, and the intrigues and corruption of courts *pretending neutrality*----that they had too little of the energy of men of busines's for the stormy times they had to steer through, and that the profligate and detestable proclamation of the Duke of *Brunswick*, (the true *proximate cause* of all the massacres and horrors in *France)*, required other antidotes than fine-spun theories and speculations, however just and excellent, I am ready to admit: nor shall I be backward in stigmatising with just epithets of abhorrence, the ferocious barbarity, the enormous, and almost unparalleled cruelty (I say *almost*----for I have not forgotten *Ismael* and *Warsaw!)* with which the more energetic party abused their power! But if it was the misfortune of *France*, that her philosophers were deficient in the powerful energies of manhood*, and her energetic characters destitute

tute

---

* "France," says Madam Roland, " was in a manner destitute of *men*. Their scarcity has been truely surprising in this revolution, in which scarcely any thing but *pigmies* have appeared.

tute of the humanising temperament of philoso-
phy, surely it is not therefore just, to attribute to
the former the favage ferocity that deformed
the latter; or, by confounding them together, to
involve the whole in one indifcriminating cen-
fure, and endeavour to bring all fcience and philofophy into difgrace, and reprefent " *knowledge*"
itfelf as " rendered *worfe than ignorance*, by the
" enormous evils of this dreadful innovation†."
Still lefs will it be admiffible, to attribute the
mifchiefs that fprung from thefe unfortunate combinations of circumftances to the principles of
the

" appeared. I do not mean, however, that there was any
" want of wit, of knowledge, of learning, of accomplifh-
" ments, or of philofophy. Thefe ingredients, on the con-
" trary, were never fo common:—but as to that *firmnefs of*
" *mind*, which J. J. Roffeau has fo well defined, by calling it
" *the firft attribute of a hero*, fupported by that *foundnefs of judg-*
" *ment*, which knows how to fet a true value upon things, and
" by thofe *extenfive views* which penetrate into futurity, altoge-
" ther conftituting *the character of a great man*, they were
" fought for everywhere, and were fcarcely any where to be
" found." Thefe obfervations difplay at once great pene-
tration and great prejudice in this extraordinary woman.
The latter prevented her from looking for *real greatnefs*
of mind beyond the boundaries of her own party ; but the former compelled her to acknowledge, that within this pale it was
not to be found. The qualities, however, of which the *Gi-*
rondifts were fo obvioufly deficient, were moft eminently pof-
feffed by feveral of the Mountain party, and by *Danton*, in particular, perhaps in as high a degree as any individual
whofe " name is deftined to live in the pantheon of hiftory."

* Letter, &c. p. 21.

the revolution, if it can be proved (and the proof
I think, would not be difficult), that *the imbecility
of the philofophic, and the ferocity of the energetic party,
had their remote caufes alike in the vices and cruelties
of the old defpotifm.*

Is Mr. *Burke* really fo ignorant, or does he pre-
fume fo far upon the ignorance of his fellow citi-
zens---upon the " ftupefaction of the dull Englifh
" underftanding*," as to pretend that the *philofo
phers* and the *Septembrizers* of France were the
fame perfons;---that the promulgators of the humane, the incontrovertible, the glorious principles
that breathed through the fpeeches and declara-
tions of the National Affembly, and enlarged, at
once, the boundaries of fcience and philanthropy,
were alfo the perpetrators of thofe horrid maffacres, and ftill more horrible executions, by which
all principles, all humanity, all juftice, were fo
outrageoufly violated? Reafon, at once, revolts
at fuch a conclufion. But, fortunately, this
argument, fo important to the human race, does
not reft upon the conclufions of fpeculative reafon. Fact----ftrong, ftubborn, incontrovertible
fact (fo hateful to the juggling philofophers of *the
old fect)* ftares us in the face fo openly, that one
knows not how fufficiently to admire the confidence of the man who could fo grofsly mifrepre-

* Letter, &c. p. 63.

K   fent

fent *events and affairs of yefterday*, or the fupinenefs
and voluntary ignorance of thofe whom fuch mifreprefentations could deceive!

Who are the philofophers and metaphyficians
of France, whofe fubtile theories of humanity,
and refinements of univerfal philanthropy, have
been fo mixed and confounded with cold barbarity, or favage ferocity, as to juftify this favourite
Claudian figure of rhetoric----" cannibal philofo-
" phy,"with which we are fo frequently indulged?
Which of the *metaphyficians of France* has been "rea-
" dy to declare," either by word or action, " that
" he did not think a prorogation of humanity for
" two thoufand years, too long a period for the
" good he purfued?---or that his imagination was
" not fatigued with the contemplation of human
" fuffering, through the wild wafte of centuries,
" added to centuries of mifery and defolation*?"

I could point out, with infinite facility, certain *Englifh metaphyficians*, who go much beyond all
this ; whofe " humanity," (and whofe liberty alfo)
may be truely confidered as " at their horizon ;
" and like the horizon, always to fly before
" them*:" who would put *Liberty to fleep*, that
fhe might be able (when they thought it
convenient) to open her eyes—preferve the
freedom of the Conftitution, by eftablifhing
defpotifm upon its ruins; fhew their hatred

* Letter, &c. p. 62.

of

of violence, by inceſſant appeals to military coercion; their love of juſtice, by ſanguinary perſecutions *iniquitouſly legal*; and their humanity, by a conſpiracy to ſtarve twenty-four millions of people: and who, ſo far from being "fatigued with the contemplation of human ſuf-"fering, through the wide waſte of centuries, "added to centuries of miſery and deſolation," wiſh for *eternal* war—*eternal* maſſacre, pillage, and deſolation;—pronounce, that peace with regicides *never* muſt be made*; and ſeem to wiſh, that when their *tongues* can no longer call for blood and carnage, "their *ſkins* may be made "into *drums*, to animate *Europe* to eternal "battle†."

It is eaſy alſo to point out metaphyſicians in this country, who anſwer too well ſome other of Mr. *Burke's* deſcriptions—who "with ‡ their ſo-"phiſtical *Rights*" (not "*of man*," it is true, but) *of rotten-boroughmongers*, "to falſify the account, and "*the ſword* § *as a make weight* to throw into the "ſcale," profeſs to have armed one part of their fellow citizens for the ſubjugation of another; and protect the freedom of ſenatorian debate, by threatening to anſwer the arguments of their opponents with the ſabres of a *prætorian cavalry*.

* Letter, &c. p. 80.   † Ibid. p. 3.   ‡ Ibid. p. 54.
§ See debates on Colonel M'Leod's motion on the ſubject of the Fencible Cavalry.

How

How gracefully appeals to humanity and vir
tue come from fuch lips as thefe! How fit and
appropriate to fuch men, the moral indignation
which burfts forth in reproaches of *Barbarifm* and
Cannibal Philofophy!

I wifh not to degenerate from argument to
abufe. I truft I have conducted myfelf throughout thefe ftrictures with a temper and moderation which will fhew, at leaft, that *Sans
Culottifm,* in its true fignification*, is not inconfiftent with the urbanity and mildnefs of polifhed
life; and I fhould be forry, towards the clofe of
my labours, to forfeit a character fo effential
to public utility: but if hard words muft be
ufed—if our adverfaries, in defect of argument,
will appeal to abufe, can it be helped if the ill
directed ball rebounds? and may it not be admiffible, fo far, to retort upon them, their *unci-
tizen-like* (or, in their own language, *ungentleman-
like)* epithets, as to afk them, whether thefe are
not the real literary affaffins—the real philofophical banditti, and metaphyfical bravoes, from
whofe example they have derived thofe extravagant
and incongruous definitions which, by a ftrange
jumble of characters and events, they endeavour,

* I beg leave to quote from the earlieft of my political
works, my own definition of a *Sans Culotte.*—" An advocate
" for the rights and happinefs of thofe who are languifhing in
" want and nakednefs." *Pol. Lect.* p. 26.

in

in their virulent rhapfodies, to apply to the *philofophers* and *literary men* of France?—But the jaundiced eye of prejudice fees every thing difco-loured, and knows not that the diftemper exifts in itfelf.

I mean not to deny that crimes and exceffes have been perpetrated in *France*. Deeds have been done " at which the face of heaven glows " with horror!" But let not Mr. *Burke* hide the deformity of his own caufe in this black cloud of indifcriminate abufe. Let him bring forth his lifts of philofophical banditti and affaffins; and let us fee this pretended connection between the *metaphyfics* " *of the new fect*," and the crimes that have torn that fometime diftracted country, or his attack upon *French principles* muft fall to the ground. If the *exceffes* cannot be proved, either logically or experimentally, to have been connected with the *principles*, coincidence of time is nothing to the purpofe, and the one cannot be faid to have produced the other. Now if the principles did not produce the exceffes, the ex-ceffes muft have been produced by fomething elfe: and nothing can be more illogical than to condemn any fet of principles on account of confequences that never refulted from them.

It matters not, I repeat it, that the principles were propounded, and the exceffes committed nearly about the fame time. If a philofopher and an affaffin happen to take fhelter at the fame inn,

is

is the philofopher therefore a cut-throat, and the affaffin a metaphyfician? But Mr. *Burke's* way of arguing is ftill more inconfiftent and unjuft.—— A banditti of ruffians, or " cannibals," if he pleafes (for I can find no epithet too ftrong for their crimes) having broken in upon a company of philofophers, who were teaching the principles of juftice and philanthropy to a throng of newly emancipated flaves, they killed and devoured the greater part of them, and then began to fall upon the pupils: and for this reafon, and for no other, (unlefs it be that the philofophers had affifted the throng in efcaping from the tyranny of their mafters) this acute logician confounds together, the devourers and the devoured; and becaufe one party were philofophers and the other cannibals, calls them a fet of cannibal philofophers.

Is not this, I demand, a fair ftatement of the cafe? Confider, I conjure you, my fellow citizens, for the queftion is well worthy of ferious examination; and it is time we laid afide our animofities and our heats, and examined it with temper and moderation. The mifreprefentations that have too long inflamed our minds " are not " wholly without an object*!" While we are waging war with Gallic Liberty, we are lofing our own. Corruption has been long affailing us

---

* Letter, &c. p. 4.

on every fide; and though her fhafts may have been fteeped in anodynes to prevent the prefent fmart, the wounds are, for that very reafon, the more dangerous. Defpotifm is now approaching with gigantic ftrides; and, diftracted and alarmed by a thoufand incoherent terrors, we are finking, for fhelter, into the vale of abject fubmiffion. But let us diffipate, in good time, thefe vifionary delufions,—thefe vapours of the drowfy brain; left, when awakened at laft upon the extreme verge of deftruction, we fhould be obliged to return by that uphill path whofe rugged acclivities have occafioned fo many ftrains and bruifes to our unhappy neighbour.

" Awake! arife! or be for ever fallen!!!"

Be not deluded by idle rhapfodies and arbitrary combinations. Exceffes and cruelties are not forms of government. Actions are not principles ---either *old* or *new*. Philofophy is not a cannibal; nor can a cannibal be a philofopher! The *new principles of France*, as they are called, are good in themfelves:—the principles of equal rights, and equal laws. They are, in fact, the *oldeft principles in the world:* the principles upon which the wifeft and happieft governments of antiquity were founded: expanded and improved, it is true, but not fundamentally altered, by the wifdom derived from the improved ftate of human fociety—the wider

diffufion

diffufionof intellectual acquirement---and the more general intercourfe of mankind.

Thefe principles, I repeat it, in themfelves are good. If our antagonifts are ferioufly of a different opinion, why do they not examine them, without mifreprefentation or abufe, on the fimple foundation of their own merits or defects? Why confound them with other things? Why pretend to difcufs principles, and talk of nothing, in reality, but the actions of unprincipled men? Is time unfteady, becaufe my watch goes wrong? Is it not noon when the fun is in the meridian, becaufe the parifh dial is out of repair? Can *principles*, which are the fun of the intellectual univerfe, be changed in their nature or their courfe by the vile actions of a few ruffians? Prove to me, by difpaffionate argument, that the *principles* of the French Revolution are falfe and pernicious, and I will relinquifh them at once, and thank you for delivering me from my errors. But while my reafon tells me that they are confonant *in themfelves* with truth and juftice, it is not calling them *French* principles—it is not calling them *new lights* —it is not *the hoary prejudice of fix thoufand years*— it is not calling me *Jacobin*, nor calling others *cannibal philofophers*----it is not talking of the " ig- " norant flippancy*" 'of a man whom the learned folidity of colleges and confiftories have never been

* Letter, &c. p. 77.

able

able to anfwer----it is not all the declamatory bitternefs of *Burke*, the metaphyfical frenzy of
Windham, the fanguinary rage of *Pitt*, nor the
long-winded fophiftry of *Scott* and *Mitford*, fhall
compel me to relinquifh thefe important truths:
----no; not though it could be proved that the
crimes of *Marat* and *Robefpierre* furpaffed the
favage wickednefs of the fiend *Zuwarrow*, and the
ferocity of Croats and Hulans.

Marat and *Robefpierre* were no more to be regarded as integral parts of *the new principles of
France*, than *Pitt* and *Dundas* as parts of *the old
principles of England*; or than the *fire of London*
as having been a part of the river Thames, becaufe its waves were blackened by the rubbifh of
falling houfes, and the blazing rafters floated
along the ftream. The rafters and the rubbifh
were fwept into the fea, and the Thames regained
its wonted clearnefs: *Marat* and *Robefpierre* are
fwallowed up in the ocean of eternity, and the
new principles of France remain; and if *Pitt* and
Dundas were to die of a furfeit, after a *Wimbledon*
dinner, I do not believe, for my own part, that
our liberties would be lefs fecure.

As men are not principles, fo neither are particular actions. Mr. *Burke* might as well con-
tend, that barracks and fubfidized mercenaries,
and the fhort memory of a minifter on a trial of
life and death, are the Britifh conftitution, as that

l.   the

the tyranny of *Robefpierre* was the new French fyftem of philofophy and politics. To come ftill clofer to the point, it were as rational to affirm, that the maffacres of Glencoe were the principles of *our* Glorious Revolution, as that the maffacres of September were the principles of the Revolution of France !

That the revolution has had its " harpies*," as deteftable as either *Virgil* or Mr. *Burke* has defcribed, who feafted on the general wreck, and were for leaving " nothing unrent, unrifled, " unravaged, or unpolluted*," there can be no doubt: nor is it neceffary, to account for the generation of " thefe foul and ravenous birds of " prey*," to defcend with the poet to the regions which fuperftition has peopled with more than mortal wickednefs; or to mount with the political declaimer to the regions of philofophy and metaphyfics.

What fort of figure *Fouquier Tinnanville* would have made by the fide of the metaphyfical Sir *John Scott*, I do not pretend to fay; but who ever fufpected either *Marat, Robefpierre, Le Bon*, or any of that fanguinary party, of vifionary fubtilties and metaphyfical abftraction? Which of thofe fine-fpun metaphyfical theories, whofe abftract perfection is fo abhorrent to Mr. *Burke's* " in- " ftincts,"—which of thofe breviaries of funda-

* Letter, &c. p. 21.

mental

mental principles which commanded the aſſent, and excited the admiration of the philoſophical world, is attributed to either of theſe men? *Robeſpierre*, it is true, was a member of the Conſtituent Aſſembly; and we find him, at an early period, in poſſeſſion of conſiderable popularity: but his popularity was not of a deſcription to claſs him with thoſe *ſpeculative literati* againſt whom the politicians of the *old ſect* have conceived ſuch an inveterate abhorrence.

However this country may be diſpoſed to indulge its vanity in compariſons, they are not always to our advantage. The *French* Robeſpierre was no *apoſtate*. There was a certain ſteadineſs and conſiſtency in his conduct and character, which, (together with ſome grand traits of ſimplicity and diſintereſtedneſs) even in the midſt of abhorrence, compel us to reſpect him. Again, I repeat it, compariſons are not always in our favour: in the character of the *French* Robeſpierre there was nothing to excite our contempt. He had vices---demons of deſolation! bear witneſs, he had vices: but they were not the vices of corruption. He neither maintained himſelf in riotous luxury, nor enriched lethargic brothers, and imbecile relations with the plunder of his country, diſguiſed under the ſpecious names of places and penſions. He had cruelty too, the thought

of

of which makes one's flesh creep: but though
he issued a decree to give no quarter to *Bri-*
tons or *Hanoverians*, found in arms, he never entered into a conspiracy ·to *starve* twenty-four
millions of men, women, and children!----He
had virtues too---grand magnificent virtues! for
" pure·unmixed, dephlegmated, defoecated evil,"
exifts no where but in the inflamed imagination of Mr. *Burke.* He was fuperior to all the
fordid temptations that debauch the little mind---
the allurements of luxury, oftentation, and rapacity. Surrounded by all the temptations of un-
limited power, he lived like a private citizen,
and he died a pauper.

Robefpierre was, however, from the firft a man
of blood. He was for giving every thing to the
people, it is true; but he was for giving it them
not by the cultivation and expanfion of intellect,
but by commotion, and violence, and fanguinary
revenge: and therefore it was that the revolutionary movements of *Robefpierre*, perhaps, in defpite
of himfelf, hurried him into the moft infufferable
of all tyrannies, inftead of conducting the people
to freedom. There can be no freedom in the
world but that which has its foundations in the
encreafed knowledge and liberality of mankind.
Tyranny comes by violence, or by corruption: but
Liberty is the gift of Reafon.

Of

Of this important truth the Revolutionary Tyrant feems to have been entirely ignorant: and from this defeƈt, and the want of perfonal courage, proceeded, I believe, all the errors and all the horrors of his adminiftration. Nay, fo far was he from that metaphyfical abftraƈtion, which places its confidence in fine fpun theories and bird's-eye fpeculations, that his conduƈt has given birth to a report, that he cherifhed almoft as inveterate an abhorrence againft philofophers and literati, as Mr. *Burke* and his new friends.---- So far was he from upholding the dangerous herefy of illimitable inquiry, that he would have roafted an atheift at the ftake with as much fatis-faƈtion as the moft pious bifhop of the church.

During the reign of his defolating tyranny, philofophy was filenced, fcience was profcribed, and daring fpeculation foared no more. France was threatened with midnight ignorance; and in the *Club of the Cordeliers,* at that time one of the inftruments of his tyranny, a motion was even made to confume the public libra-ries.

Away, then, with thefe fhallow pretences for degrading the nobleft exercife of human intelleƈt. Away with this idle jargon of cannibal philofo-phers and literary banditti! So unnatural an alliance never yet was formed; nor ever will. The affaffins and ruffians of every clime, whether

in

in the pay of *regular* or *revolutionary* tyrannies, have a fort of univerfal inftinct whifpering to them, that knowledge and oppreffion cannot thrive together.

" If we do not filence the prefs," fays *Woolfey*, " the prefs will filence us:" and *Robefpierre* (a little wifer in this refpect than *Edmund Burke)* prohibited, in the Jacobin Club, the publication of his own fpeeches; left his intemperance fhould provoke difcuffions which his tyranny could not afterwards controul.

But though the pretences of Mr. *Burke* for confounding together the *philofophy* and the *crimes of France* are thus completely refuted, I do not expect that the ground will be abandoned. It is too important a part of the permanent confpiracy againft the liberties of mankind to be readily given up. Remove but this delufion from the eyes of the people, and the reign of Corruption could not laft---" no, not for a twelvemonth." The principles of liberty are fo confonant to the general good---the caufe of the rotten borough-mongers is fo deftitute of all rational fupport, and the miferies produced by that fyftem are fo numerous, that nothing but the groundlefs terrors fo artfully excited---nothing but the prejudices infpired againft all fpeculation and enquiry, by confounding together things that have no connection, could poffibly prevent the people of Britain fhouting from every village,

village, town, and ftreet, with one unanimous and omnipotent voice—

" REFORM! REFORM! REFORM!!!"

Of this the faction in power are fufficiently aware; and therefore it is, that their hatred and perfecution are principally directed, not againft the furious and the violent, but againft the enlightened and humane. Therefore it is, that they endeavour to confound together, by chains of connection flighter than the fpider's web, every fanguinary expreffion, every intemperate action of the obfcureft individual whofe mind has become diftempered by the calamities of the times, not with the oppreffions and miferies that provoke them, but with the honeft and virtuous labours of thofe *true fons of moderation and good order* who wifh to render their fellow citizens firm and manly, that they may have no occafion to be tumultuous and favage; to fpread the folar light of reafon, that they may extinguifh the groffer fires of vengeance; and to produce a timely and temperate reform, as the only means of averting an ultimate revolution. Thefe are the men againft whom the bittereft malice of perfecution is directed. Thefe are the men againft whom every engine of abufe and mifreprefentation is employed; to calumniate whom their " Briton," and their " Times," and their dirty Grub-ftreet pamphletteers, are penfioned

out

out of the public plunder—and againſt whom grave ſenators from their benches, and *penſioned Cicero's* from their literary retreats, are not aſhamed to pour forth their meretricious eloquence, in torrents of defamation, and to exhauſt all the fury of inventive (or *deluded)* malice. Theſe are the men for whoſe blood they thirſt; and whom they endeavour to deſtroy by new doctrines, not only of accumulative and conſtructive treaſon, but of *treaſon by ſecond ſight :* making them accountable for actions they were never conſulted upon, books they never read, and ſentiments they never heard. Theſe, in ſhort, are the men for whoſe deſtruction laws are perverted, ſpies are employed, and perjurers are penſioned: and when all theſe artifices prove inadequate to the end, theſe are the men to ſtop whoſe mouths bills have been propoſed, in parliament, ſubverſive of every principle of the conſtitution, leſt the nation at large ſhould be in time convinced that they are not what they have been repreſented: but that *the friends of Liberty and Reform, are the true friends of Humanity and Order!*

This would be, indeed, a terrible diſcovery for thoſe who are ſupported by corruption : and in this point of view one cannot blame them for the ſelection they have made of the objects of their perſecuting hatred. To let their vengeance fall at once upon the really violent, would be an

act

act of impolicy, that would shew them " to be
" foolish, even above the weight of privilege
" allowed to wealth*" and power. Were these
suppressed (arguing upon their own supposition,
that persecution can suppress) what would become of those pretences by which, alone, they
have rendered the advocates of reform obnoxious
to the fears, and consequently to the hatred, of the
alarmists? But if they could destroy the real reformers, the men of reason, of humanity, of intellect, they would destroy the magnets (if I
may so express myself) around which, whenever
their influence shall become sufficiently diffused
through the intelligent atmosphere, the good
sense, the spirit, the virtue of the country, must be
attracted ; and when it is so attracted, and when
the parts shall firmly and peacefully cohere, and,
thus brought under the influence of the true laws
of nature, shall press together, with the united
force of attraction and gravitation, to one common centre of truth, the seven days work of crea-
tion is complete---the system is restored to order;
and the unruly tempest of tyranny and corruption
shall endeavour in vain to prolong " the reign of
" chaos and old night:" the planet shall roll on,
regardless of the storm---grace, beauty, fertility,
happiness, shall flourish in full luxuriance, and

the meteors of delufion fhall burft and expire. But were this principle deftroyed---were thofe powers of intellect and virtue by which, alone, this grand harmony can be produced, fuppreffed by the timely interference of fuperior power, and every thing left to the mifguidance of thofe *ignes fatui* of intemperance and revenge, which, in the night of ignorance, a foul corrupted atmofphere never fails to ingender, in the low, rank, marfhy fens of vulgar intellect, the friends of liberty would be no longer formidable; but while they floundered about in a thoufand wild directions, deftitute of any common principle, and unconfcious whither they were going, muft prefently be fwallowed up in the bogs, and fwamps, and quagmires of their own delufion.

In fimpler language, though commotion and violence are the watch-words of alarm, it is the progrefs of reafon---the power of prefiding intellect, of which, in reality, the borough-mongering oligarchy ftand in dread. This, they are juftly apprehenfive, may in time diffeminate what they call its *infectious influence*, fo far as to palfy the very hands of corruption, and caufe the fceptre of their furreptitious authority to fall, by the mere operation of its own weight, from their enfeebled grafp. But as for actual violence---this they can defpife: ---this, fome parts of their conduct, and many of their fentiments, would almoft lead one to fufpect

pect them of being defirous to provoke. Their
military, they may fuppofe, would quickly fupprefs any infurrection; the tumult would afford
a convenient opportunity of ridding the country
of obnoxious individuals*; and, while the victo-
rious fword was yet out of the fcabbard, who
could blame them, if they took the opportunity
of organizing a *military defpotifm ?* But the friends
of liberty are aware of this; and their conduct
has proved how little they deferve the calumnies
of Mr. *Burke*, and the minifterial faction. Intemperate language may fometimes have been ufed,
and even received with intemperate applaufe;

---

* I underftand that a certain officer, of fome rank in the
army, has avowed that inftructions of this kind have been given:
"If any tumult fhould arife," he is reported to have faid, " we
" know our game. We fhould not fpend our fury on the *rabble*,"
(fuch is the language they ufe towards thofe ufeful members
of fociety, whofe induftry fupports and feeds them!) "we fhould
" look out for thofe prating rafcals, * * * * * * *, and make
" fure of them, wherever they were to be found." I fhall not
infert the names that were placed at the head of this black lift
of profcription, for more reafons than one. Suffice it to fay,
they were fuch as fully to juftify the above chain of reafoning.
They were not men of blood—not men of violence—not men
who yelp for tumult or revenge; who call out for rebellion,
or breathe forth flaughter. No—no:—fuch characters are
fafe (for the prefent). They are the neft eggs : the hen phea-
fants, whom the keen fportfman muft fpare, that they may
breed frefh game. Let us hope, however, that this was only
gafconade: a *military bounce:* and that human nature is not
yet fo depraved, that fuch inftructions could be either given
or accepted.

M 2   but

but the voice of reafon has always been the com-
manding voice; nor could the groffeft infults,
nor the moft methodifed attempts of treafury
hirelings, police ruffians†, and minifterial fanatics,
(for there are fanatics, it fhould be remembered,
of all fects) ever throw them into confufion, or
provoke them to violence.

But Mr. *Burke* would be ill qualified for a
champion in behalf of that caufe he has *now*
undertaken to fupport, if he could not confound
together the clear and obvious diftinctions between intellectual firmnefs and tumultuous vio-
lence---the energies of the mind, and the energies
of the dagger! Ill would he be calculated to
fupport the tottering caufe of oligarchy and corruption, if he could not divert popular attention from the abufes and violence of his own
party, by exciting unmerited odium againft all
intellect and enquiry, and throwing upon the
philofopher and the philanthropift the imputation
of thofe crimes which the enemies and perfecutors
of thofe characters in reality perpetrate, whether
in France or Britain.

The fophiftries, however, and mifreprefentations
of my antagonift end not here. Not only has he
confounded together characters and events that

---

† For a ftriking illuftration of the propriety of this expreffion, fee " Narrative of Facts," prefixed to " Political Lectures,
vol. I. part I. p. xii. and xiii."

were in reality diftinct--not only has he charged
the crimes of a few ferocious ufurpers upon a
whole people, and made the philofophers of
France the authors and promoters of that very
fyftem of cruelty, in refifting which fo many of
them loft their lives; but he has affigned the
exceffes and crimes of the revolution *altogether* to
a wrong caufe; and charged upon *republicanifm* the
guilt of ingendering thofe hideous propenfities—
thofe enormous depravities of gigantic wickednefs, which nothing but *defpotifm* ever did, or ever
can produce. His talent feems, indeed, to lay
quite in this way. In his " Reflections," in
defiance of the well-known fact, that the famine,
or *great fcarcity of bread*, was one of the princi-
pal caufes of the revolution, he charged the
revolution with having produced that famine. I
am not, therefore, furprifed to find him ftill
obftinately perfifting in charging all thofe cannibal difpofitions upon the Republic, and the
Rights of Man, which could not have exifted at
all, if the old defpotifm had not generated them;
and which, at any rate, the revolution would only
give their proprietors an opportunity of difplay-
ing in deeds of open violence and commotion,
inftead of employing them to perpetrate the
fecret cruelties and affaffinations of the court—
in devaftations fanctioned by *regular authorities*,
and oppreffions " *iniquitoufly legal!*"

That

That popular commotions call all the vices, as well as the virtues of the community into action, cannot be denied. That when " the cauldron of " civil contention" is boiling over, the foulest ingredients will fometimes be at the top; and that, in the general fermentation, combinations the moft deleterious will fometimes be formed, no reflecting man has ever yet denied. It is an additional argument why the rulers of the earth fhould take care not to render fuch commotions neceffary and inevitable.

Happy, thrice happy fhall it be for thofe princes and governments, who derive a ufeful leffon from the events that have paffed before us! Happy, thrice happy fhall it be for thofe wife and moderate rulers, who, in this bufy, changeful, and enquiring age, put not their trufts in *janiffaries* or *Swifs Guards*; but, adopting the falutary advice of the great Lord *Verulam,* fhall illuftrate by their conduct that profound and falutary maxim, that " the fureft way to prevent fedition " is not by fuppreffing complaints with too much " feverity, but to take away the matter of them.*" In other words, the beft way to manage the diftemper, is not to amputate the limb but to remove the caufe.

* Effays, Civil and Moral, p. 77. and 80. *edition* 1725. Title —*Of Seditions and Troubles.* Query, Why has Mr. *Burke* overlooked this effay!

But

But whatever vices and difpofitions the heat of
popular commotion may call into action, muft
have been generated by former circumftances.
Extraordinary exigencies place men in ftrong
lights, and fhew them fuch as they are: but they
do not create characters of a fudden; nor manu-
facture mankind anew. Revolutions are touch-
ftones for the real difpofitions; but they do not,
like the whifp of a harlequin's fword, change the
dove into a tyger, or the tyger into a dove.
If, therefore, we were to admit that all the revolutionifts—the whole body of the French people,
were indifcriminately involved in the guilt of
thofe exceffes fo exultingly quoted, and fo wickedly exaggerated by the foes of liberty—what
would be the conclufion? Where would the
blame in reality fall, but upon that old fyftem of
defpotifm, for the reftoration of which Mr.
Burke " would animate Europe to eternal battle."

The revolution in France, or more properly
fpeaking, the philofophers and patriots who firft
fet the *new order of things* in motion, did not create
their agents. They did not fow the earth (like
Cadmus) with dragon's teeth, and reap a harveft
of men to carry on their projects. They were
obliged to make ufe of the inftruments already
made to their hands; and when the game was on
foot, the bad as well as the good would have
their fhare of the play. If, to refume the allufion,

a race

a race of contentious homicides did burft from the ground, and alternately deftroy each other, the feed was fown by the *old defpotifm*, not by the *new philofophy*.

Mr. *Burke*, indeed, himfelf feems confcious, that the wild and ferocious charaĉters he declaims againft, could not have been formed by the revolution---he knew that *the men whom he ftigmatizes for projeĉting and forming the Republic, could not have been formed and educated by the Republic.* Unwilling, therefore, to aſſign, in plain terms, the generation of the monfters he defcribes to the right caufe, he calls in the aid of poetry, and tells us, that thefe " revolution harpies, fprung from " night and hell, and from chaotic anarchy, " which generates equivocally all monftrous, all " prodigious things."---True, Mr. *Burke*, I thank you for the allufion. The revolution *harpies* did fpring, moft aſſuredly, from what with claſſical precifion of metaphor you have called *hell*, and *night*, and *chaotic anarchy*. They fprung, indeed, from that hell of defpotifm, into the very abyfs of which *France* had for whole centuries been plunged---They fprung, indeed, from that night of ignorance in which the beft faculties of the human mind had been fo long enveloped and extinguiſhed---They fprung, indeed, from that chaotic anarchy of vice, licentioufnefs, profligate luxury, and unprincipled debauchery, into which the

the morals of the country had been thrown by the influence and example of the court, and which, it is rightly faid, *generates equivocally all monftrous, all prodigious things!* Thefe were, indeed, the infernal fources of all the evil: and but for that " night, that hell, that chaotic anarchy," of the old defpotic fyftem, fuch " obfcene harpies,"---fuch " foul and ravenous birds of prey," never could have been in exiftence, to " hover over the " heads, and foufe down upon the tables," of the revolutionifts, and " rend, and rifle, and ravage, " and pollute, with the flime of their filthy offal," the wholefome banquet, which the philofophers of the revolution had occafioned to be fpread for the focial enjoyment and fuftenance of mankind.

Such *were* the monfters generated in the infernal region of the old tyranny; and in fuch regions fuch monfters always *muft be* generated, till effects fhall ceafe to be commenfurate to their caufes, and nature's felf fhall change. Was it not time then, think you, that this " great deep" were broken up---that the chaotic mafs of tyranny and corruption might be thrown into new motion, by the addition of fome frefh principle, or ftimulus, by means of which (through whatever noife and uproar) a more wholefome arrangement might be produced---

" And from confufion bring forth beauteous order?"

It

It is in vain to tell me, that thefe harpies were no harpies to mankind till they fhewed themfelves as fuch. Defpotifm had always its harpies: and they were always well banqueted. They banqueted in filence, indeed, under the *old fyftem:* they were not garrulous, as under the *new order:* nor did the prefs trumpet forth their attrocities. But they rent, and ravaged, and rifled, and polluted, and devoured, and acted all their horrors and abominations, with avidity and diligence enough, for centuries before the revolutionary fyftem was fet in motion. Of this Mr. *Burke,* and every man who is travelled, either in climes or books, is well informed. They had their public theatres, in which they tore the quivering limbs of their prey, for the amufement of courtly fpectators; and they had their cages—their cells—their Baftiles, or, as Mr. *Burke,* more delicately calls them, " king's " caftles *," where they might banquet in filence, and riot undifturbed in all the horrid luxuries of cruelty. The revolution gave them nothing but a voice: and this attribute was ultimately beneficial: for their hideous fhrieks and yells, and the audacious publicity of their cruel ravages, concentrated, at laft, the general hatred of the country they infefted. They were hunted to their caverns; and the race has become extinct.

* Reflections, &c.

I do

I do not, however, mean to affirm that the harpies of the new fyftem were the fame individuals as would have been the harpies of the old: though, in many inftances, it was probably the cafe. Cruelty is cruelty, under whatever fyftem it acts; and an inquifitor, a Fermier General, and the prefident of the revolutionary tribunal, in the *reel* of political mutation, might join hands, turn round, and change pofitions *ad infinitum*, without ever appearing out of place.

But this is not all. Inhuman oppreffion generates inhuman revenge. All ftrong impreffions produce ftrong effects. That which we paffion-ately deteft, we are fometimes in as much danger of imitating, as that which we paffionately admire. How often does the hatred of cruelty degenerate into the very thing we abhor? How often does the hatred of tyranny render men moft tyrannical? —for the hatred of tyranny is one thing—the love of liberty is another. The former is a common inftinct; the latter is the nobleft attainment of reafon. Add to which, that *lex talionis* is, with the generality of mankind, the law of moral action. " Eye for eye, and tooth for tooth," is inculcated as the mandate of Deity. But the nobility and clergy of France, had not eyes and teeth enough to anfwer this account. Can we wonder at what enfued ?

It

It would have been well for France, if the influence of the old tyranny upon the moral cha-racter of the people, had terminated with the evils here enumerated. If the cruelty of long-esta-blifhed oppreffion had only made the irritable ferocious, and the ignorant revengeful, thefe deftructive paffions might have been controul-ed by the energy of more cultivated minds, till they had been foftened and humanized by the influence of more favourable circumftances. But tyranny had not left to the revolution the poffi-bility of the crime with which Mr. *Burke* has charged it in a former pamphlet. It had " flain " the mind* of the country" long before that revolution took place. Literature, it is true, had been highly cultivated. Science had been libe-rally patronized, in the upper circles; and even that republican talent, *eloquence*, had been che-rifhed with a diligence moft important, in its ultimate confequences, to mankind. But the jealous nature of the government—the terrors of the Baftile----the fhackles of an imprimatur---- the homage exacted by birth and fortune, and, above all, the frivolity and effeminacy of cha-racter impofed on the nation by a profligate, thoughtlefs, and luxurious court, which, having

* Reflections, &c.

nothing

nothing manly in itfelf, could not be expected to
tolerate manhood in its dependants, " dwarfed
" the growth" of that mental energy which thefe
taftes and ftudies could not otherwife have failed
of producing. Hence originated the circumftance of which the female citizen *Roland* com-
plains, that the revolution produced no *men*. The
courfe of ftudy had been perverted by the influence of the government. The clofet of the
philofopher was infected by the contagion of the
court. Solidity was facrificed to ornament----the
virtues to the graces. In acutenefs, fubtility, pene-
tration, and even profundity, their literati were not
deficient: but they wanted that boldnefs----that
active energy----that collected, unembarraffed,
firmnefs and prefence of mind, which nothing
but the actual enjoyment of liberty, and an unre-
ftrained intercourfe with a bold, refolute, buftling,
and difputatious race of men can poffibly confer.
This energy of mind, without which it is impoffible, in any ufeful and important fenfe of the
word, to be a man of bufinefs, muft be fought
among " thronged and promifcuous audiences,"
" in theatres and halls of affembly;" for there
only it is to be found. The philofophers of
France, however, from the neceffities under which
they were placed by the government and inftitutions of the country, either mingled with the gay
circles of the diffolute and great, and became infected

fected with fervile effeminacy, or indulged their
fpeculations in a fort of fullen retirement, where
the mafculine boldnefs of the true philofophic
character was chilled by folitary abftraction.

Thus did the genius of the old defpotifm deftroy, alike, the humanity of the bold, and the
energy of the humane and enlightened. And
thus it was that, the philofophers being feeble,
and the men of intrepidity being ferocious, the
republic was torn and diftracted by the crimes
which the defpotifm had prepared.

If it were neceffary to ftrengthen this argument
with hiftorical evidence----if it were neceffary to
prove by particular records, that the difpofition .
to thefe inhuman crimes did not originate in the
nature and influences of *republican government*, we
might appeal to the *maffacres of St. Bartholomew*;
to the barbarous oppreffions and wanton cruelties
defcribed by *Arthur Young*, in the firft edition
of his travels, as fpreading mifery and defolation through the lordfhips and feigniories of
what Mr. *Burke* calls " the *virtuous* nobility of
" France*;" and, above all, to the inhuman pu-
nifhments---the favage protraction of lingering, but
exquifite tortures, with which inventive cruelty,
in fome notorious inftances, gratified the appe-
tite of royal vengeance. Nay, whatever might

---

* Letter, &c. p. 49.

be

be the conduct of particular leaders, rendered cruel at firft by their intolerant zeal, and afterwards, ftill more fo by their dread of retribution, it would not be difficult to prove, that *the character of the people* was *humanized* and *improved*, inftead of being rendered more ferocious by the influence of the revolution. I appeal, in particular, even to the very circumftance of the decree, that no quarter fhould be given to the *Britifh* or *Hanoverians*. What was the confequence of that decree? The brave foldiers of the republic refufed to execute it, even in an individual inftance; and the dictator was obliged to recal a mandate which he found himfelf unable to enforce. Would the foldiers of the old defpotifm, who perpetrated the horrors of the night of St. Bartholomew, have fo refufed? Did the military flaves of our good ally, the Emprefs, difplay the fame obftinate repugnance to a ftill more inhuman order? Let the ghofts of murdered babes and fucking mothers, that ftill hover unappeafed over the captive towers of *Ifmael* and *Warfaw*, anfwer the folemn queftion!

Having thus replied to the arguments, or rather to the abufe, of Mr. *Burke*, againft the revolutionary philofophers of France; and having fhewn, in the firft place, that the cannibals and the philofophers were not only diftinct, but oppofite, fets

of

of men; and, in the next, that the cannibalifm
proceeded not from the revolution but from the
old defpotifm; it is not neceffary to examine,
very elaborately, the truth of his affertion, that
" every thing in this revolution is new." If my
arguments are juft (and they are advanced in the
very fincerity of my heart) it is matter of little
confequence whether every thing is new, or every
thing derived from ancient precedent. All that
I fhall do, therefore, is to quote from *Machiavel*,
his brief abftract of the caufes and progrefs of revolutions, that the reader may fee how far the
obfervations of that fine hiftorian and acute poli-
tician will countenance this bold affertion.

" At the beginning of the world," fays this
author, " the inhabitants being few, they lived
" difperfed after the manner of beafts. After-
" wards, as they multiplied, they began to unite,
" and, for their better fecurity, to look out for
" fuch as were more ftrong, robuft, and valiant,
" that they might *choofe* one out of them to make
" him their head, and pay him obedience*."—
He then briefly fketches the progrefs of fociety
to another ftage, when the people having emerged
in fome degree from barbarifm, " being to make
" an *election of their prince*, they did not fo much

---

* Difcourfes on firft decade of Livy, Book I. chap. 2.

" refpect

" refpeét the ability of his body, as the qualifica-
" tion of his mind, *choofing* him that was moft
" prudent and juft. But by degrees their go-
" vernment coming to be hereditary, and not by
" eleétion, according to their former way, *thofe*
" *who inherited degenerated from their anceftors, and,*
" *negleéting all virtuous aétions, began to believe that*
" *princes were exalted for no other end but to difcrimi-*
" *nate themfelves from their fubjeéts by their pomp,*
" *luxury, and other effeminate qualities* ; *by which*
" *means they fell into the hatred of the people, and,*
" *by confequence, became afraid of them*; and that
" fear encreafing, they began to meditate revenge,
" opprefling fome and difobliging others, *till*
" *infenfibly the government altered, and fell into ty-*
" *ranny*. And thefe were the firft grounds of
" ruin, *the firft occafion of conjuration and confpiracy*
" *againft princes*; not fo much in the pufillanimous
" and poor, as in thofe whofe generofity, fpirit,
" and riches would not fuffer them to fubmit
" to fuch difhonourable adminiftrations. The
" multitude following the example of the nobi-
" lity, took up arms againft their prince; and
" having conquered and extirpated that govern-
" ment, they fubjeéted themfelves to the nobility,
" which had freed them. Thefe detefting the
" name of a fingle perfon, took the government
" upon themfelves; and, at firft (reflecting upon
" the late tyranny) governed according to new

O   " laws,

" laws, devifed by themfelves, poftponing parti-
" cular profit to public advantage; fo that both
" the one and the other were preferved and
" managed with great diligence and exactnefs.
" But *their authority afterwards defcending upon*
" *their fons, who, being ignorant* of the variations of
" fortune, as not having experienced her incon-
" ftancy, *and not contenting themfelves with a civil*
" *equality, but falling into rapine, oppreffion, ambition,*
" *and adulteries,* they changed the government
" again, and brought it from an Optimacy to be
" *governed by a few, without any refpect or confidera-*
" *tion to juftice or civility: fo that in a fhort time it*
" *happened to them as to the tyrant: for the multitude*
" *being weary of their government, were ready to*
" *affift any body that would attempt to remove it.*
" By thefe means, in a fhort time, it was extin-
" guifhed: and forafmuch *as the tyranny of their*
" *prince and the infolence of their nobles were frefh in*
" *their memory, they refolved to'reftore neither one nor*
" *the other,* but concluded upon a popular ftate."
Such then is the brief abftract, drawn by the maf-
terly pen of *Machiavel,* of the origin, progrefs, and
revolutions of political fociety: and though fome
particular inftances may be marked with partial
varieties in one feature, and fome in another, fuch
is the general picture which the hiftories of the
revolutions of the moft celebrated nations of the
ancient and modern world exhibit. The leffon it
teaches

teaches is moft important. Well would it be for
the rulers of the earth, if they would lay the inftruction to their hearts; and inftead of producing by one
fort of revolution the neceffity of another, would
pay that *refpeft* to the liberties of their refpective
countries, which they are fo anxious to exact
towards their own perfons and authority. It is
true, that in the ftyle and language of hiftory, in
general, there is but one fpecies of revolution,
fpecifically marked as fuch—the revolutions by
which governments are overthrown: but if we
ferioufly attend either to this abftract, or to the
hiftories of the nations, of which it is fo juft a
fummary, we fhall find that thefe have uniformly
been preceded by revolutions of another kind—
the revolutions by which governments become
tyrannical.

In one refpect then, at leaft, and that the moft
important of all—in refpect to its caufes, there
was nothing like novelty in the French Revolution: nothing that could furprife or aftonifh us.
The *pomp, luxury, and effeminacy of the court* had
been long notorious. The extravagant and profligate diffipation of the princes, their *neglect of
all virtuous actions,* and their indulgence in every
vice, was a common theme of reproach againft
them, through all the nations of Europe. The
fanguinary and vindictive fpirit of the laws, the
rapine, oppreffion, and jealous tyranny of the govern-
ment,

ment, and the confequent mifery and deftruction of the people, (in this country at leaft) were become proverbial; and *flavery and wooden fhoes* was the logic by which we juftified our hatred of the French nation*. Surely thefe were caufes enough to juftify a revolution----caufes enough to produce one. The only aftonifhment muft be, that it did not come before.

The only novelty in this event, as far as relates to caufation, confifts in the circumftance of the nobility and the monarchy being overthrown together. But this very circumftance fhews the profundity of *Machiavel*, and the accuracy of his reafoning; and expofes the " flippancy". of Mr. *Burke*. It is novelty of combination in the hiftory of facts; but not novelty of combination in the hiftory of caufe and effect. It is an additional argument in fupport of the affertion, that popular revolutions are confequences of the revolutions of tyranny and oppreffion. In *France*, two† revolutions took place at the fame time; becaufe two† kinds of tyranny domineered together, and therefore two † revolutions were neceffary. The

---

* And yet, now we are to hate them for throwing their flavery and their wooden fhoes away !!!

† I might fay three. But I omit the ecclefiaftical tyranny, becaufe it does not fall immediately in the way of my argument; and becaufe the fame reafoning will evidently apply in this inftance as in the others.

nobility,

nobility, by " their natural ignorance, their indo-
" lence, and contempt of all civil government*;"
and ftill more by their unbounded rapacity, their
wanton infolence, their barbarous exaftions, and
all-defolating pride—or, in the language of my
quotation, by *the rapine, oppreffion, ambition, and
adulteries*, which they indulged *without refpeft or
confideration of juftice or civility*, had brought themfelves into general abhorrence and deteftation,
even before any *conjurations and confpiracies againft
the prince* had arifen. They had made themfelves
partners in the guilt, and were therefore partners
in the punifhment of the tyranny. Inftead of
being a bulwark between the prince and the
people, to preferve the latter from the oppreffion
of the former, they were indeed the chief battery
from which the deftruftive engines of Gallic
tyranny fpread ruin and defolation through the
land.

And are thefe the perfons whom Mr. *Burke*
pretends " are fo like the nobility of this country,
" that nothing but the latter, probably not fpeak-
" ing quite fuch good French, could enable us
" to find out any difference†?" I would not for
the whole penfion of this " defender of the order,"

---

* Montefq. Spir. Laws, b. ii. c. 4.

† Letter, &c. p. 59. Mr. *B.* it is true, applies the comparifon only to the Duke of *Bedford*; but it applies either to all
or none.

that

that this comparifon fhould be true: for if it were
—if the titled great of Britain were what thofe
of France have been, then fhould I exclaim, in
the bitternefs of my foul, that their crimes and
their oppreffions ought no longer to be endured
—no longer protected by the laws and inftitutions of the land; but that they, alfo, in their
turn, ought to be driven into ignominious banifh-
ment.

Never---never (let us hope) will our nobility
and great proprietors realize the fimile Mr. *Burke*
has fo imprudently made! Never---never (let
us hope) will the vices, the profligacy, the info-
lent oppreffion, and immeafureable rapacity of
the French ariftocracy, ravage and depopulate
this country: for if they fhould, not all the rhapfodies of penfioned eloquence---not all the treafon
and fedition bills of *Pitt* and *Grenville*, can avert
the terrible cataftrophe.

But the danger to this country comes from
another quarter. It is not from the ariftocracy,
properly fo called, that we have moft to dread. It
is not even from the prerogatives of the executive
power. It is from the oligarchy of the rotten
borough-mongers. It is from the corruption of
that which ought to be the reprefentative branch
of the legiflature. This it is that is undermining
(I muft not fay has undermined) the conftitution
and liberties of Britain. This it is that is realizing,
with

with fatal rapidity, the prophefy of *Montefquieu---*
" As all human things have an end, the ftate we
" are fpeaking of will lofe its liberty. It will
" perifh. Have not *Rome, Sparta,* and *Carthage*
" perifhed? It will perifh, when the legiflative
" power fhall be more corrupted than the exe-
" cutive*!"

Such, at leaft, are the apprehenfions that have
crowded upon my mind. Such are the dangers
which, during the laft five years, I have endeavoured, with the moft laborious diligence, to avert,
by the only means through which they can be avert-
ed—by provoking popular enquiry; by roufing, as
far as I had power to roufe, the energies of peaceful but determined intellect; and by endeavour-
ing, with all the little perfuafion I could mufter,
to wean my fellow citizens from the prejudices
and delufions of party—from all idolatrous attachment to names and individuals, and to fix
their hearts and affections upon principle alone---
the great principle of philanthropy---the principle
of univerfal good---the fource and fountain of all
juft government--of *equal rights, equal laws, reciprocal refpect, and reciprocal protection.*

Thefe are the principles I have endeavoured to
inculcate, in political focieties, at public meet-
ings; in my pamphlets, in my converfations, and

in

* Sp. Laws, book xi. c. 6.

in that lecture-room, (that school of vice, as Mr. *Burke* is pleased to call it) at which he is so anxious to dissuade the " *grown* gentlemen and " noblemen of our time from thinking of finishing " whatever may have been left incomplete at the " old universities of this country *."

If to have inculcated these principles with a diligence and perseverance which no difficulties could check, no threats nor persecutions could controul---if to have been equally anxious to pre-serve the spirit of the people, and the tranquillity of society---to disseminate the information that might conduct to reform, and to check the intem-perance that might lead to tumult---if these are crimes dangerous to the existence of the state, the minister did right to place me at the bar of the Old Bailey: and, if perseverance in these principles is per-severance in crime, it may be necessary once more to place me in the same situation of disgrace and peril. If to assemble my fellow citizens for the purpose of political discussion---if to strip off the mask from state hypocrify and usurpation---if to expose apostacy, confute the sophisms of court jugglers and ministerial hirelings, and drag forth to public notice the facts that demonstrate the enormity and rapid progress of that corruption under which we groan, and by means of which *the rich are tottering on the verge of bankruptcy, and*

* Letter, &c. p. 35.

the

the poor are sinking into the abyss of famine---if this is to keep a public *school of vice and licentiousness* *, then was it right in ministers to *endeavour* to seal up the doors of that school with an act of parliament; then was it right that I should be held up to public odium and public terror, by the inflammatory declamations of the *Powises* and *Windhams*, the tedious sophistries of the *Scotts* and *Mitfords*, the virulent pamphlets of the *Burkes* and *Reeveses*, and the *conjectural defamations* of *Godwin* †. But upon what sort of pretence, even the inflamed and prejudiced mind of Mr. *Burke*, can regard me as " a wicked pander to avarice and ambition ‡," I am totally at a loss to conjecture. I have at-

---

* Letter, &c. p. 36.

† It is painful to see such a name, in such a list. But if men of great powers, however sincerely attached to liberty, voluntarily, by cold abstraction and retirement, cherish *a feebleness of spirit*, which shrinks from the creations of its own fancy, and a solitary vanity, which regards every thing as vice, and mischief, and inflammation, but what accords with its own most singular speculations; and if, under these impressions, and regardless of the consequences to an isolated individual, assailed already by all the malice and persecutions of powerful corruption, they will send such bitter defamations into the world, as are contained in the first 22 pages of " Considerations on Lord *Grenville's* and Mr. " *Pitt's* Bills," they must expect to be classed with other calumniators. The bitterest of my enemies has never used me so ill as this *friend* has done. But nothing on earth renders a man so uncandid as the extreme *affectation* of candour.

‡ Letter, &c. p. 47.

P   tached

tached myfelf to no party. I have entered into none of the little paltry fquabbles of placemen and oppofitionifts, by which, alone, profit or promotion can be expected. My heart and foul, it is true, and I believe the heart and foul of every man who entertains one grain of refpect for the rights and liberties of mankind, was with the *Whigs* in their conduct and fentiments relative to two bills, to which, as they are now paffed into laws, I fhall give no *epithet*. I truft they have an epithet, fufficiently defcriptive, engraved upon the heart of every *Briton*. I thought, and I ftill think, that the man muft be extravagant, indeed, in his expectations, who was not fatisfied with their behaviour in this refpect; and particularly with the firm and manly oppofition of *Fox*, *Erfkine*, and *Lauderdale:* from the firft of whom, I confefs, I did not expect a conduct fo bold and *unequivocal*. If any thing can preferve the party from that perdition into which, by its *cold, half meafures*, it has fo long been falling, it is perfevering in the temper, fpirit, and fentiments of *that* oppofition. So long as they do perfevere in that temper and fpirit, I hope, and truft, that the hearts and fouls of Britons will continue to be with them. So long as they do fo perfevere, my heart and foul, for one, will be with them, moft undoubtedly:---not as a *partizan*, for that I abhor---but as one who, coinciding with them in a particular

principle,

principle, is anxious to neglect no opportunity
by which that principle can be promoted. But if
ever, which, I truft, will not be the cafe, they
ſhould be again weighed down by the pondrous
millſtone of that fort of ariſtocracy already de-
ſcribed*, which ſo long hung round their necks,
and prevented them from ſoaring to the heights
of confiſtent principle, INNS and OUTS, WHIGS
and TORIES, will become once more objects
alike of indifference---of contempt!

Thus, then, I have coincided, upon a particular point, with men from whom, upon other ſub-
jects, I have widely diſſented; and I have even
perſuaded myſelf, that if thoſe men perſevere in
the ſentiments and conduct diſplayed on that oc-
caſion, the introduction of Mr. *Pitt's* and Lord
Grenville's bills will ultimately prove to have been
proud days for *Britain*. But amidſt theſe feelings,
I have forfeited no confiſtency. I have ſhrunk
from no principle. I have become no " pan-
" der to avarice and ambition:" nor have I
courted the patronage of wealth or greatneſs, by
relinquiſhing any particle of that independance,
which does, indeed, render me " prouder by far"
than all that frippery " of the Herald's College,"
which Mr. *Burke*, ſo ſcientifically, details †; in
as much as the pride of manly principle is ſu-

* P. 24 to 27.　† Letter, &c. p. 39.

P 2　　　　　　　perior

perior to the infantile vanity of the age of toys and baubles.

Neither have I facrificed to intereft nor gratified avarice, by my particular purfuits: whatever the narrow-minded and the envious may fuppofe. What I have received from the public, as the voluntary price of my labours, has been fpent in the public caufe :—in redeeming myfelf from the incumbrances produced by inceffant perfecutions; in alleviating (where I could) the fufferings of other victims; and in the expences with which my exertions have been attended. I may fay of my politics as *Goldfmith* of his mufe,

" They found me poor, and ftill have kept me fo."

But though I murmur not at this, neither fhould I hold myfelf a " pander to avarice and " ambition," if I had really been enriched by my lectures. Whatever emolument I might have reaped, furely I alfo might have faid, " I have not " received more than I deferve* :" for affuredly every man deferves all that he can get by the honeft exercife of his faculties, whether of mind or body. To increafe the burthens of an almoft ftarving people, by receiving penfions from the product of public taxes, may be bafe. To extort money, under pretence of propagating doctrines which thofe who *muft pay* are neither defirous to

* Letter, &c. p. 10.

promote

promote nor willing to hear, may be a fpecies of public robbery: but to derive fupport, *however liberal*, from a courfe of public inftruction, to which *the only perfons who pay are the voluntary pupils*, Mr. *Burke*, if he had fucceeded to that profeffor's chair, of which, it is faid, he was once ambitious, would certainly have been ready to prove, not only blamelefs, but honourable.

If avarice and ambition had been my ruling paffions, it is furely admiffible for me, " thus " attacked," to fay, that with my talent for public fpeaking, I fhould not have abandoned, from fcruples of principle, the profeffion of the law; which lays open fo fair a field for the gratification both of the one and the other. If felfifh principles actuated my conduct, I needed not the infinuating meffage of a man (whofe eminence in a learned profeffion ought to have lifted him above the fhameful office of a *go-between to male proftitution)* that, " if I chofe, I might do fomething better for " myfelf than delivering public lectures." Even without adopting thefe words in a fenfe which, coming from fuch a quarter, I fuppofe them to convey---even without becoming what my calumniator has called me---" a pander to avarice and " ambition;" I have fome confidence in my own refources; and I perfuade myfelf, that with my habits of induftry, and with my little ftock of reputation, I *could* derive a better fubfiftence from

fome

some of the profitable branches of literature, than my politics ever brought me, or ever will bring.

If I have any motives of perfonal intereft, I deceive myfelf, and am a fool. If I were to regard myfelf alone, I believe no act of parliament could affect my interefts: and certainly no intereft----no reward can compenfate me for the ravages upon my conftitution, and the facrifices of focial enjoyment (which, as a hufband and a father, conftitute the deareft gratifications of my foul), occafioned by thofe exertions in which I have been fo inceffantly and laborioufly employed. But how fweet and alluring foever the bloffoms of domeftic felicity, we muft not, in the felfifh enjoyment of cur own gay *partierre*, neglect to root out the thorns from the road of the way-faring traveller, who is too heavily laden to ftoop and remove them for himfelf.

I have, therefore, renewed my exertions; and, although an act of parliament has prohibited lectures " on the laws, conftitution, government, " and policy of *thefe realms*," have opened my fchool again, and fhall continue to open it, at fuch intervals as health will permit, to give lectures on the laws, conftitutions, government, and policy of *other* realms, which it is not yet prohibited to difcufs; to inveftigate the *elements of political fcience*, and trace the *caufes and confequences of the various revolutions which the tyranny and oppreffions*

fions

fions of various governments have in different ages pro-
duced: and though I profefs no infallibility----no
patent of exemption from occafional flights, or
rather *flounderings,* of verbofe nonfenfe, I think I
may venture to promife that "no *grown* gentle-
" man or nobleman," who fhall be defirous " of
" finifhing," at *Beaufort-buildings,* " any thing that
" may have been left incomplete at the *old* uni-
" verfities*," will lofe his time in liftening to
fuch jargon as the following paffage, with the
expofition of which I fhall clofe this pamphlet.

" I conceived nothing arbitrarily, nor propofed
" any thing to be done by the will and pleafure
" of others, or my own; but by *reafon,* and by
" *reafon* only. I have ever abhorred, fince the
" firft dawn of my underftanding, to this its ob-
" fcure twilight, all the *operations of opinion,* fancy,
" inclination, and will, in the affairs of govern-
" ment, where only a *fovereign reafon,* paramount
" to all forms of legiflation and adminiftration,
" fhould dictate. Government is made for the
" very purpofe of oppofing that reafon to will,
" and to caprice, in the reformers, or in the re-
" formed; in the governors, or in the governed;
" in kings, in fenates, or in people †!"
In the name of common fenfe how many gods
has Mr. *Burke* in his mythology?---Who is this

* Letter, &c. p. 35.   † Ibid. p. 24.

Sovereign

Sovereign Reafon? In which of the feven heavens does fhe refide? For he has told us that in this blind world fhe is no where to be found! At firft, indeed, I fufpe&ted my antagonift (for whom no incongruity, no contradi&tion is too glaring) of having flipped unawares, into rank democracy; and of defcribing, by this *new Gallicifm---Sovereign Reafon,* the colle&tive reafon of the SOVEREIGN PEOPLE; or, in other words, the concentrated opinion of mankind: but upon looking a little further, I find that this cannot be his meaning, for he exprefsly fays, that " government is made " for the very purpofe of oppofing this [Sovereign] " Reafon (whatever it is) to will, and to caprice, " in the reformers or in the reformed, in the " governors or in the governed, in kings, in " fenates, or in people:"---that is to fay in all human beings. Now that which is to oppofe the will and caprice of all human beings (or even to decide, in oppofition to all human beings, what is *reafonable,* and what is *wilful* and *capricious)* muft be either pofitive, exifting *inftitution,* or it muft be fome *being* who is more than human. That it cannot be pofitive, exifting inftitution, which is to be regarded as the ftandard, is evident; becaufe Mr. *Burke* talks of " reformers " and reformed;" and, *if pofitive exifting inftitution is the ftandard of Sovereign Reafon, there can be no reform at all;* for every attempt to reform is,

upon

upon this hypothefis, an oppofition of the will
and caprice of the reformers (whether king,
fenates, or people) to this Sovereign Reafon.
What was this reafon, then, which was not the
operation of the opinions either of others or his
own, but without confulting which he neither
conceived any of *his* reforms, nor propofed any
thing to be done?---Why does he thus bewilder
our judgment, without amufing our imagination?
Why leave us benighted in thofe cold fogs of
myfticifm? If he is inclined to impofe upon
us a belief in fomething more than mere vulgar
human faculty, by which his reforms, and the
all-perfect wifdom of government, are to controul the will and caprice of the human race,
why not ftrike us at once with fome grand flight
of inventive fancy, that we may at leaft have
fomething pleafurable and amufive in exchange
for the common fenfe we are to furrender. Could
not *Numa Pompillius* have lent him his *Egeria?*
or *Socrates* his *Dæmon?* or St. *Dunftan* his red
hot tongs, to lead the devil about the country, for
the amufement of gaping ruftics?'

Of all the fictions, romances, and impofitions,
that bewilder mankind, the moft infipid, as well
as the moft abfurd, are thefe dull, canting, metaphyfical rhapfodies!

The reader will judge between us; but for my
own part, I have ever confidered reafon as no-

Q   thing

thing more than one of the operations of the mind, employed in the refearch, comparifon, and digeftion, of that knowledge by which folid and ufeful underftanding can alone be produced. For the fanity or perfection of this faculty, I have always confidered that there is no pofitive teft or ftandard; and that the moft confident deduction of the moft cultivated reafon is but " an opinion" ftill; except in as much as relates to that *one fcience,* which is known to admit of demonftration. Confidering, therefore, that all queftions of government, muft ultimately be decided either by the aggregated *reafon* (or as Mr. *Burke* may call it, the aggregate *will* or *caprice)* of fociety, or, as is more commonly the cafe, by the reafon, will, or caprice of the governors; and, confidering, alfo, that the multitude can have no intereft in reafoning wrong; I have thought it of the higheft importance to awaken my fellow citizens, in this time of peril and affliction, to the exercife of their faculties on queftions of the greateft importance to us all; and to inculcate, not as matter of dogmatical opinion, but of ufeful enquiry, fuch fentiments and doctrines as to me appeared conducive to public happinefs. This, notwithftanding the calumny and perfecution with which I may be affailed, I fhall ftill continue to do, not rafhly, I hope---I am fure not

fearfully;

fearfully; varying my means, according to the circumftances under which new impediments and new reftrictions may place me. Among other things, I have thought it my duty to make fome reply to this feditious and inflammatory libel of Mr. *Burke* (for fo to me it appears in the moft eminent and alarming degree;) making it, at the fame time, a vehicle for the inculcation of principles favourable at once, I believe, to the *Rights of Man* and the *interefts of humanity*---for they are indeed body and foul, and can only exift together.

I would fain hope that this pamphlet, and the anfwers it has provoked, and will provoke, may roufe, once more, that general fpirit of enquiry, fo effential at this time; and that notwithftanding the temporary panic produced by the new treafon and fedition acts, we fhall return once more to the manly and vigorous exercife of thofe innumerable means, which ftill lay open for enforcing the bold enquiries of reafon, and the facred love of humanity and juftice; that thus, if the wild and defperate projects of the minifter fhould unhinge the fyftem he profeffes to fupport, and produce that diffolution of all focial bonds, which he profeffes fuch anxiety to avert, the *principle of order* may ftill remain, indeftructible, in the hearts, feelings, and paffions of my fellow citizens;

citizens; and (as Dr. *Darwin* fo beautifully fays of *Nature*, from the rude mafs, in which he fuppofes Death, and Night, and Chaos, will fometime or other mingle the whole planetary fyftem)

" High o'er the wreck, emerging from the ftorm,
" Immortal *Freedom* lift her changeful form;
" Mount from the funeral pyre on wings of fame,
" And foar and fhine, another and the fame!"

FINIS.

www.ingramcontent.com/pod-product-compliance
Lightning Source LLC
Chambersburg PA
CBHW032102010726
47493CB00008B/2492